"A startling new take on a classic—
Carissa's modern retelling of *Mrs Dalloway* is
both intensely moving and deeply perceptive."
—Cheryl Julia Lee, author of
We Were Always Eating Expired Things

"This novel is a generous homage to place as
well as a tribute to the art of attention which
is capable of revealing a whole life in a single
moment—which we might call a kind of love."
—Lawrence Lacambra Ypil, author of
The Highest Hiding Place

If It Were Up to Mrs Dada

If It Were Up to Mrs Dada

A NOVEL

CARISSA FOO

EPIGRAM BOOKS
SINGAPORE · LONDON

Epigram Books UK
First published in 2018 by Epigram Books Singapore
This Edition published in Great Britain in April 2020
by Epigram Books UK

Copyright © 2020 by Carissa Foo
Author photo by Chong Yew. Used with permission.
Cover art by Michelle Tan
Design by Joanne Goh

The moral right of the author has been asserted.

All characters and events in this publication, other than those clearly in the public domain, are fictitious and any resemblance to real persons, living or dead, is purely coincidental.

All rights reserved. No part of this book may be reproduced, stored in a retrieval system, or transmitted by any form or by any means, mechanical, photocopying, recording or otherwise, without the prior permission in writing of the publisher.

A CIP CATALOGUE RECORD FOR THIS BOOK
IS AVAILABLE FROM THE BRITISH LIBRARY.

ISBN	978-1-91-209851-4
PRINTED AND BOUND IN	Great Britain by Clays Ltd, Elcograf S.p.A. Epigram Books UK 55 Baker Street London, W1U 7EU

10 9 8 7 6 5 4 3 2 1

www.epigrambooks.uk

For Sarah

How happy I was if I could forget
To remember how sad I am
Would be an easy adversity
But the recollecting of Bloom

Keeps making November difficult
Till I who was almost bold
Lose my way like a little Child
And perish of the cold.

—Emily Dickinson

I

Mrs Dada said she would buy the flowers herself.

For Lulu had her work cut out for her. The tables had to be set; the men from Neo Garden were coming. And then, thought Cheryl Dada, what a morning—

What a fucking hot morning. For so it had always seemed to her that clouds would gather when it was the hottest, that some draught would hover over the home, that the heavens would open. But now, sniffing the warm, sultry surroundings, she was sure there was no cool air to plunge into. "Doesn't smell of rain," Cheryl Dada said to herself, staring up at the sky. "No chance of rain today," she said again. Sweat was dripping down her back. Cotton—or not? Cheryl Dada thought, rubbing her right palm against the baby blue pants that were sticking to her thighs. Probably not, though it certainly wasn't chiffon either. Chiffon was the cream panel top she put on for today. Sleeveless and light, it was supposed to keep her cool. But it was not airy as advertised. "Fuck *AIRYSTOCRACY!*" Mrs Dada said, biting the words, as she remembered the slogan plastered on the window display—*FEEL HIGH AND LIGHT*! She should have guessed as much that airy meant nothing in this equatorial climate. With crossed arms and a strong neck, she stood on the porch, waiting for a breeze.

Mrs Dada did not see this coming: the heat; the cloudless sky; the air that was thick with haze. Her plan was to go to Ang Mo Kio Hub to buy an assortment of flowers but that would be too arduous now, especially in this heat, alone, without Lulu, who was busy laying the tablecloths. No, Mrs Dada had decided, she would not leave the sheltered porch—not under this searing sun, not over her dead body. The weather forecast had said it would be cool. Cool, she thought, meant a walkable weather. But where was the breeze? Where was the cool? Today was anything but cool.

The weather report could have been "Thunderstorms expected tomorrow" or "Heavy showers in the morning". The man on the television could have said it would snow; he could have said hail or typhoon or cyclone. He could have thrown out some weather jargon that nobody would understand. He could have said something curious, something extraordinary. But to say cool temperatures tomorrow... Cool temperatures! What the hell was that—in Singapore anyway? That was a weak lie, utterly thoughtless. It was the kind of lie not worth telling, not even worth exposing. If it were big enough, Cheryl Dada thought, if it were far-fetched enough, it would cease to be mere lie and become a front page story: *Thunder Strikes Boy Swimming in Bedok Reservoir. Snowfall in Singapore for the First Time. Avalanche on Bukit Timah Hill.* But no—Cheryl Dada was certain of this—no story was ever spun from cool temperatures. Well, not in Singapore.

Come to think of it, most stories begin with lies. Most lives could be lies, Mrs Dada thought, looking into the distant blue. Lies with truths far away, far far away, then one day they become the real thing. A lie told long enough has its own life. Kudos to those who buy the truth; but she would rather a big fat lie. A good lie, she meant to add. A big, fat and good lie (note: not the same as a white lie) is a story of its own—original and unfettered by moral rectitude, relieved of the obligation to truth.

The weatherman's greatest fault was telling a half-hearted lie that bored its way to nowhere. That's the worst kind of lie, Cheryl Dada thought. No wonder he's reporting the weather.

Anything would have been better than this underwhelming fib about today being cool when they had announced during morning assembly that it was 34 degrees. "Damn it!" Cheryl Dada let out as she wiped the sweat off her forehead. She should have known better than to trust a man in spectacles and a suit. That's the typical conman's dress code, she thought to herself. Remember when that curly-haired man locked her in the guest room? He was in a handsome checked shirt too, looking decent until he held her wrists and insisted she and he were lovers!

Mrs Dada had trusted the weatherman and she was feeling the effects of the blunder; her skin was reddened by indignation and injustice. The rising anger was saved by a split second of confusion: was she mad at him? Or at herself for believing—again? Why was she so gullible? History is wont to repeat itself, though never in exactly the same way. If all heroes must have a tragic flaw, Mrs Dada's was that she was too trusting.

While people are generally suspicious about strangers, particularly the ones lurking gingerly outside the MRT stations with red files tucked under their arms, Mrs Dada would entertain the unfamiliar men who came up to her, young punks in suits with stiff, glossy hair who eventually left her as eager as they found her; the woman was insufferable, they thought, asking too many questions and wanting elaborate answers to every one of her questions: "What's the difference between accident and hospitalisation plans?" "What's the global fund all about?" "Why do insurance companies like the colour red?" Each answer, which they thought was enough to satiate the auntie, was merely an appetiser; it was a prelude to desultory conversations of corporate conspiracies, government policies—and if they were lucky, she'd digress to more conversational topics like the CPF Act and the Retirement Sum Scheme.

Mrs Dada had a listening ear that was enthusiastic even when nothing substantial was being said. Too often she devoured facts—be they half-facts, hearsay, headlines—and spun them into solid stories, carrying all of them in her heart as though they were her own. And once she was persuaded into one belief, she bit hard and found it impossible to let go. To this day she still could not believe that Lee Kuan Yew had died. The man was immortal to her—that was the first truth and nothing else could supersede it.

It was a dark, extremely dark day when the news broke. Cheryl Dada was mostly kept in the isolation room that evening. She was so lost and listless that she picked up the paper that John Pitts had slipped under the door and wrote just below the words "Automatic Thought": *Death*. "Alterative Thought": *The dark age is here. Nobody is coming to save. Not the British or Japanese. Not the Singaporean.* In the column titled "Emotion or Feeling", she scribbled offhandedly: *DÉJÀ VU*. She remembered struggling to write properly because her wrist was sore and there was no light.

Thinking back, the events of the day still seemed surreal to her. It was a lie—April Fool's had come early. She was certain that whatever coffin they had prepared, the cavalcade of black cars, the lachrymose crowd on the TV were part of an elaborate hoax; the body lying in the Istana was not his. "NO!" Cheryl Dada screamed in the TV room, hurling curses at the CNA news reporter. "NO, IT CANNOT BE!" she exclaimed, and flung the remote control across the room when he first announced LKY's death on primetime morning. She broke into a fit, her body shaking, madly convulsing as Daniel and the nurses rushed into the room and tried to hold her down. (Lulu still had the scars from the tears in her skin. Three curved marks on her left arm.) Cornered and pinned to the floor, she thought she was losing it; but anger turned her into a deaf beast, and since she could not hear them, she saw only the fluttering hands and mouths opening and closing as if they were fish gulping for air. All this pushed her over the edge. Cheryl laughed and laughed at them. She could not stop until she had been brought to the room and there was nothing to see and laugh at because the room was dark.

It was a traumatic day for Cheryl Dada and those who were around her. She who first believed that Harry—yes she called him Harry—was like Dracula and those pearlescent-skinned vampires who fed on blood for immortality could not believe otherwise. Harry had been there from Day One—what was the nation going to do without him?

The death of the Senior Minister, who had also been the first Prime Minister, the only Minister Mentor and once the Secretary-General of the PAP, haunted Cheryl Dada. The following nights she started to have nightmares about exoduses and invasions. She dreamt that a tsunami hit Marine Parade and swallowed all of their reclaimed land; that Malaysia had cut their water supply and they had to collect rain water with jerrycans and drink water that was yellow like urine; that the angry swordfish were back with a vengeance and had mutated into a bionic species whose laser bills could destroy guns and rifles, much less tree trunks. For weeks she worried over the nation's predicament and her own future, about what would happen to them. For without Harry, Singapore was a nation of lost sheep, bleating for this and that, horrified and hungry. The only leader they knew, he was and still is the father of the nation; the godhead.

They were a young nation—half a century old! Just children! Then again, her father had passed away when she was barely two and she survived. So it'll be okay, Cheryl consoled herself, people will get over it; people always do. Forgetfulness is resilience in some sense. We will survive, and we have survived. Still, taking the first step into the second half of the century without Harry felt wrong to her. It was unthinkable, almost sacrilegious.

Poor Cheryl Dada was hounded by the guilt of the living. PM Lee II had declared a seven-day period of mourning for the nation to remember their founding father; Cheryl tried her best to not forget too. Every day she stared at the pictures in the newspapers, detailing his heavy eye bags, the slight creases of his forehead, the waxen skin, the tuft of hair—wispy and white like the feathers in her pillow—as if that would bring him back. Yet the more she stared, the more she cauterised his face from her memory. For a long time after, try as she might, she could only conjure the face of Bela Lugosi.

Cheryl Dada's version of the nation continued to crumble in the aftermath of his death. So great was her horror, when she found out that lions were not native to Singapore, that she did not bawl but sat unnervingly quiet at the corner of the dinner table. "Maybe elephants," someone yelled out; "Definitely not lions," said another. But wasn't the Merlion a caricature of the first lions that had roamed the land? More important, if there were no lions, then what was the Merlion? What was that thing spitting water into the Singapore River?

The talk about lions transpired over dinner some weeks after LKY's passing when Ling Na distributed a tin of Merlion cookies for dessert. It looked funny: the shape was rectangular and it was a frontal view of the Merlion's head.

Strange to not see the Merlion from its side. Strange to see only its feline head. Cheryl complained that it did not look like the Merlion; the others insisted that the Merlion could be that—it could look like anything.

The chattering went on; each woman fighting to have her voice heard. "The real Merlion nobody see before, okay—" began Loudspeaker Leow, but could not finish; her mouth was full of cookies. Felicia Phua, the youngest at the table, pasty-faced, murmured something about Asian lions. Someone—her face was blocked by Mrs Rohan—was throwing out questions: "How you know?" "Who say?" "You see before meh?" But it was Siew Eng who was winning because she had a geographical mind: "Singapore is an island surrounded by water leh, a fishing village; we are super coastal. How did the lions come here—swim ah?" Cheryl Dada would have gladly conceded to that point, but Judy Chua had to add, "Wah lau mai siao lah. Merlion where got real? Yeong tao nao sio lah. Don't be stupid, can?"; a fucking mean thing to say. Facts were facts, and Cheryl Dada accepted that. But calling her stupid was a personal attack. God, she hated that woman; she hated her whooping voice.

Finally, Ling Na had to intervene. It was her fault, no doubt; she was the one who had brought the Merlion cookies. Like a judge with her gavel, she banged the tin on the table and there was order. "The Merlion is a story," she began. "Singapore, like many other countries, whether big or small, needs a story," she continued, blabbering on about

Qin Shi Huang and the terracotta army, Hou Yi and Chang Er, Yue Lao and his red strings and how Sun Wu Kong conquered the West. Some of the stories were mythologies, some about the art of war, others were romances. The story was whatever the people needed.

The faces at the table brightened up, as if they had been enlightened. "Yah hor! No wonder!" The voices started again and boomed through the dining hall.

The women chomped on the sugar-free cookies. Cheryl Dada sat silent at the end of the table, her mind still ruminating on the point of stories. She sort of understood: the Merlion was like China's Green Dragon. It was also the Centaur, the Minotaur, Medusa.

Still, the truth about the Merlion did not sit well with her. She could not be persuaded by Ling Na's Chinese references. In her heart she fought the explanations. For Cheryl Dada, trusting as she was, had long chosen the first tale. For although she believed easily, she only believed once. History could not be wrong; the origin of the nation was irrefutable. Sang Nila Utama beheld the chimera; Singapura was a Malay fishing village. It was Malaya, not Malaysia.

The Merlion must have been a species of its own, she concluded. It had to exist, if not what was Singapore? If there were no Singapore, was she still Cheryl? The Merlion had to exist; it had to be real. And Cheryl Dada believed it was real. The certainty of her thought pleased her; but the smile departed as soon as she remembered that she was supposed to get the flowers.

There was no breeze; no cool temperature.

"Not a cloud in the sky got the fucking sun in my eye," Cheryl Dada hummed to herself, squinting against the light that filled the creases on her face. "Argh! This fucking sun! Why is it so fucking hot?" she groaned, raising her hand to shield her eyes from the cruel glare of the sun.

The hard consonant struck her ear. So what? Mrs Dada reflected silently, tugging at her chiffon top, fanning herself. So what if she used a couple of bad words here and there? As if people in the neighbourhood were saints. No one was squeaky clean here—for example, Siew Eng on the third floor of block A threw her cigarette butts, sometimes still lighted, out of the window. Evidence of her misdemeanour was found in the flowerbeds, the lettuce patch, the herb garden, everywhere except the bin.

Like in most homes, there were a lot of pent-up frustrations and wandering emotions that surfaced every now and then. They found their way into an elbow shove, a sudden push, an uncaused fight, a false accusation, a fire alarm going off. (That did actually happen when one resident attempted to suffocate herself to death by locking herself in a room while burning a basket of letters.) It was one reason why the doctors and social workers insisted on incorporating art therapy into the residents' schedules, citing to Management studies that showed it would help to channel negativity into canvases and slow down the onset of mental diseases. Their selling point was that the big private homes like St Luke's and Red River Valley used such therapy and therefore they should too; Management agreed. The residents were mostly happy about having an extra option of activity to choose from. However, Cheryl was sceptical about art classes, unconvinced that emotional expression could be taught and curated into square blocks of scribblings and ugly splashes of colours. For a moment or two she thought about Choon Eng's purple sea that was hanging, on a nail, on the main wall of the lobby.

What was Choon Eng thinking about when she painted that? Cheryl wondered meditatively, remembering the droopy eyelids that veiled the woman's pretty black eyes. They were eyes that reflected the weariness of one whose brightness had been robbed by youthful afflictions, eyes that saw the world as regal and peace-loving despite what they've had to see.

Choon Eng's sea was iridescent purple. Perhaps it was the cataracts that had turned the reds muddy. Perhaps she had imagined a version of the red sea—she used to be religious and wore an ostentatious gold crucifix around her neck. Or perhaps it was the sea that had asked to be painted. The waves were accentuated with spikes to show that the waters were ever moving; the outline was made bold in a red shade of purple, almost maroon, as if the sea were impenetrable. Over and over the paintbrush swept across the surface of the canvas producing a thick and uneven patch of sky with melding hues of purple and pink. Because Cheryl had inspected the painting countless times, she could roughly separate the purple sky from the purple sea. But it seemed to her that ambivalence was good and the division was unnecessary. Purple is as red as pink to the dead anyway.

Whether art therapy was advantageous to the old folks was disputable. What was supposedly really helpful were the geropsychologists: John Pitts and Barbara Smart. They were the expats with professional expertise hired to increase the quality of residential life. But they only came in thrice a week and knocked off exactly at five when they did. They were not available in the middle of the night, when help was most needed. Sometimes there would be wails in the wee hours of the night and then they would stop before one could identify the source; sometimes the sound of glass shattering woke the home and then it would cease as abruptly as it began. Those who were nosy and agile would hurry out of their rooms and find no commotion. The whole place was suddenly and serenely empty of noise. Not even the sound of people snoring. Rage was real but hushed. The home was hushed.

For better or worse, it was Judy Chua who would break the eerie silence of the night and the peace of the day. Hers was a high-pitched and grating voice that could cut through the wooden doors and pierce you in the temples, causing many to roll their eyes when she spoke. Judy Chua—they called her Chor Lor—lived on the ground floor of block A. It's A for Apricot, though some say it's A for Atas; yet Judy Chua was neither sweet nor uptown. She was, however, powerful—powerful enough to secure a prime room with a small private garden in the most expensive block. At 81 she had rank and years on her side. She could do no wrong, and she did no right. Her mouth was a terror—and it was not just the blatant spitting of phlegm on other people's shoes. Cursing was her way of talking: her punctuations, accents, exclamations. What angered Judy Chua the most was if someone looked her way and the eyes lingered. Even to a look of adoration, she would throw back a death stare and start cursing. "Kan ni na kua si mi?" Her mouth would widen as she spat the words: "Kua si mi lan chiao?" as if to devour completely the transgressor.

"That woman swears like a trooper," said Cheryl Dada to herself, shaking her head at the thought that they lived in the same block. Even Judy Chua's gestures were vulgar. Once she had grabbed a broom to hit at Juwel, who was trimming the grass patch outside her door, and did not stop until the nurses strapped her down. Chor Lor… Was that Teochew? Boy, did she earn her name.

The spiralling thoughts brought Cheryl Dada to the firm conclusion that she was not the worst of the lot. She might not be a saint but she was nowhere as uncouth and disrespectful as Judy Chua, and not nearly as inconsiderate as Chin Siew Eng. And even if she were as bad as people thought, at least she wasn't the only one. People ought to remember that. Not all old people are the same, Cheryl thought to herself. The word left a nauseating residue in her mouth.

"Ou…ouh…" she shaped her lips as if to whistle a tune. Although the topic of age was not taboo in the home, it was seldom discussed because it was dull. Age, to many adult women, after all, is a relative and pointless calculation.

In the home, there were women in their fifties, sixties, seventies, eighties, a handful in their nineties, and three centenarians. Quite unlike in the garden-variety old folks' homes, there were a good number of residents in their forties, a couple in their late thirties even. Felicia Phua, for instance, was 40 and Siew Eng had turned 43 last week. They weren't *old* old, certainly not as old as Auntie Ah Luan or Mrs Rohan; they were just damned enough to be here.

Felicia, plagued with severe kyphosis, who had been in a wheelchair since she was 33, was known around the neighbourhood as the Hunchback of Ang Mo Kio. As for Siew Eng, the woman was a one-legger: her right leg had been amputated after a freak car accident on the winding slope of the Cameron Highlands. Still more damned: Felicia used to be a competitive runner in school and Siew Eng, a tour guide. Both had relied a great deal on their legs. Thank God, they had met in the home and bonded through prayers to Saint Servatius—the patron for those with foot troubles.

Much like Cheryl Dada, they were women whose lives became associated with those of the invalid, damned, handicapped, infirm and spouseless. Regardless of age, they all gathered in the home. The three of them were part of the small minority, barring the Malay and Indian ladies. They were the English type who preferred to say "fuck" and "shit" and "damn it", and watched *Wheel of Fortune* instead of Channel 8 soaps. Nothing like the other Chinese women who spoke Hokkien and Cantonese, and who swore just as much, if not more.

Cheryl stood by the conclusion that she was not the most vulgar one in the home. Besides, English could never sound as crass as Hokkien. But her face grew solemn as she contemplated this more: for how could someone be vulgar when she mostly spoke Hokkien? To say she was vulgar would be racist—or "dialectist". If so, was it right of them to call Judy Chua Chor Lor? Was it right of them to call her geh ang moh? Why did they assume she spoke Mandarin and Malay? Some even thought that she knew Indian—she had to correct them: "Indian is the ethnicity. Tamil is the language," and then clarify that she did not speak Tamil. But their faces remained bewildered, others suspicious.

Unlike those who spoke dialects—and there were many in her generation—Cheryl Dada only knew English. She could manage a bit of Teochew, as much as her grandmother had taught her, a few words in Mandarin and Malay; but Hokkien she could not speak. Her grandmother told her it was unladylike. "Ah Le, you don't be chor lor like them ah," she warned. "Better don't be like them." Cheryl never knew exactly who "they" whom her grandmother spoke against were. Sometimes they were the rowdy neighbour boys, sometimes they were the hawker uncles.

Anyhow, she promised her grandmother that she would not be like them. She had never sworn while the old lady was alive. It was only after her arrival at the home that Cheryl began to pick up the curses. For one abides in the colonial language, not swear in it. Unless it was "bakero", which was the exception, because her mother had used it all the time. She said the Japanese were always shouting "bakero"; they came knocking at her door and spat "bakero" at her mother when she let them in. That they shouted "bakero" when they left her crying. Cheryl had always thought her mother was quoting the soldiers verbatim. It was only when she was older, after taking a survey course in Asian History, that she realised what her mother had been trying to tell her. She understood then the grit in her mother's voice when she told her those bedtime stories, the swift hand that switched off the radio whenever "Sukiyaki" came on.

"Damn this sun!" said Mrs Dada, feeling the heat wrapping around her. Her fringe was falling onto her forehead; half a can of hairspray was not enough to hold her hair on this muggy day.

Also, the haze was back. The news said the PSI reading was 70. That was a lie, for Cheryl Dada smelled the char in the air. Looking up at the vacuous sky, she felt an impulse to pray. The old habit returned carelessly to her. She found herself searching the sky for signs of a divine being, someone who would make it rain, provide shelter and refuge from the tireless sun; but the firmament hung detachedly above her, mostly clear and blue. No sign. No God; nothing came, as usual.

Cheryl Dada wanted many things in her life. But recently she had been latching on to the littlest things—as though she could be easily pleased. For instance, she had been all excited about learning French earlier this year. Daniel had told her that everyone was given a $500 credit to pick up a new skill ("It's a government initiative to help develop the best in us," he said), and she immediately decided that it would be a language. But not Korean—which was what most of the women in the home wanted to learn. Cheryl never got into those cheesy Korean soaps like the rest of them. She would rather spend the afternoon walking aimlessly than sit through one episode of people crying and falling ill and dying in car crashes. Wasn't the world dead enough, the home depressing enough? She could not understand why so many people would crowd in the TV room for romance. Neither could she understand why Clare was into Korean dramas when the fair-skinned, chiselled men did not interest her.

If Cheryl Dada were to learn a language, it would most certainly be French. Much to everybody's surprise, two other women were also interested. Lulu was too, but she did not count because she was neither a resident nor Singaporean. Cheryl Dada was suspicious of Felicia and Siew Eng; she thought that they only wanted to get out of the neighbourhood. The younger ones often had the most mischief up their sleeves. Some aunties called the pair Che Lun Jie Mei: Felicia was always itching to relive the thrill of speed, while Siew Eng would sit herself in any vehicle just to get a lift out to buy cigarettes.

Even though three names were put down, Daniel warned her that it was going to be difficult to get people to sign up for something as exotic as French; in fewer words, she should not get her hopes up. He explained to her that Management would not want to arrange transport for only three people and they did not have the funds to bring in instructors to conduct the classes. He was right: plans for the French class fell through. It was about practicality; nothing personal. He was right again: nothing's personal here.

If Management really wanted to talk about practicality, then what was practical about giving a woman like herself $500 in credit? She'd much rather have the cash. Exactly how practical was it for her to learn something? Daniel suggested dance: "It's trendy and fun. Be an active ager!" He gave her a list of courses including hand jive, Chinese fan dance and ballroom dancing, but it was clear he included those only because they were convenient. The Chinese dance group met every Tuesday in the multi-purpose hall and the hand jive class rehearsed in the common room of block B on Wednesday mornings. There was less paperwork, fewer arrangements to be made if she took up dance. Daniel's optimism must not be confused with genuine concern, although Cheryl could not deny that he was one of the feeling ones. She was thinking about how he had kept yawning and scratching his eyes so that no one would notice that he was tearing up at Choon Eng's service.

"The little things…" she mumbled, putting her hands together. "God, I would like some clouds," she said. It seemed the most practical thing to ask for; and if practical enough, it might be granted to her. All Cheryl Dada wanted this very moment as she stood on the porch was some relief. She wished the sun would go away. Clouds would be very nice; a drizzle would be nice too—anything to freshen up the lazy afternoon. It should rain soon; there's no such thing as drought in this country. Was that why the old specky said cool temperatures expected? Was he calling it into existence? Perhaps they were going to make it rain with those calcium salt things.

Argh, this fucking heat, Cheryl Dada let out in her mind. No way she was going to walk to the garden today. No way she was going to pass by potty-mouthed Judy Chua to get to the other side. No way she was going to get into a fight today.

"No, I'm not getting the flowers," Mrs Dada said, looking over to Lulu, who was busy setting up the tables in the parking lot. Her feet were starting to sweat.

At this moment a couple of passing clouds smudged the blue sky. Funny how they had sneaked in and filled up the sky, and the air was suddenly cooling down. Even so, the sun seemed to be chasing her with a dogged pertinacity. It made her peachy skin flare up and her lips dry. On days like today, Mrs Dada thought resignedly, even the clouds don't help.

And, she thought with conviction, she could not brave the heat for the flowers, for she would not be able to stand it. Anyway, the Hub was too far and her only escort was ignoring her. The other option was the garden. It was reasonably near and she did not need permission to go on her own. Also—and this was probably the best part about today—she had the freedom to roam around and could spend more time in the garden or her room because the hourly care plan was not enforced on public holidays and special occasions.

Still, Cheryl thought, if she were to make her way to the garden, near as it was, she might develop a rash from walking under this sun. Her skin was easily irritated lately and she had had enough of those antihistamines—they made her sleepy all day.

Examining the pink patch near her right elbow, Mrs Dada thought about eczema and melanoma, but decided the rash was too mild to be an augury of cancer. There was neither blood nor suspicious moles. It could not have been acne, she persuaded herself. Surely she was past the age for that. Must remember to ask for QV, she noted silently. And prickly heat powder too.

Looking to the parking space tucked away in the corner of the driveway, it occurred to her that transport might also be an issue. Her ride was giving way—well, it was technically her mother's; Cheryl Dada had inherited it when her mother acquired one of those motorised wheelchairs. The wheels were wonky; the seat cushion was wearing thin. She must remember to get Lulu to see to it. This time she would ask for a brand-new one, preferably American. No more second-hand stuff, she promised herself. Definitely no more bakero Japanese brands.

But it was not up to her. The actual purchase was subject to Management's approval and its preposterously long red tape. They took weeks to go over simple forms and urgent requests, forgetting that time was not a luxury in the home. Many of the residents still remembered Auntie Ah Luan. She had been the first of them, in the home for 29 years, respected for her seniority and life experiences, loved for her unflagging warmth and generosity—especially for her never-ending supply of Khong Guan biscuits that she always gave away freely. Auntie Ah Luan was a typical genial granny: small, slightly hunched, had white hair tied up in a bun and wore a pair of silver-rimmed glasses. Though she carried a hypertensive heart and the cartilages in her joints were wearing away, she never had the slightest hint of fatigue or bitterness.

An image of Auntie Ah Luan staggering along the garden path slowly came to Cheryl Dada, vivid as if it had happened yesterday. She was one of the first people whom Cheryl befriended; Ah Luan was a dear auntie and confidante to her. The 93-year-old lady loved nature and the sun; weeding was her favourite thing to do in the afternoon. The joy of working in the garden was what propelled her to put in the request for mobility aid in the first place, even though she was shy to use a wheelchair. "Jin pai seh, jin siu li," were her exact words. The garden, all for the garden.

Management took so long to process the purchase. They claimed that they needed to send for a qualified assessor to evaluate her condition before approving the request for an assistive device. Couldn't they see that ageing was not a social problem but a sentimental one? For God's sake, the old lady was confined to her bed! She could not move her legs—what more proof did they need?

Auntie Ah Luan spent her last days in bed. She did not get to smell the pandan she planted or feel the warmth of the sun. She died in her sleep, in a room without a view. The wheelchair arrived two days later and was allocated to Mrs Rohan.

The lesson was loud and clear. Auntie Ah Luan's death reminded the rest of the residents that time was not on their side. Their Casio watches synchronised to a common time beeped on, with or without their owners. The hours of decay pursued them to the fatal climax, the clock soldiered on after each denouement.

Even though Mrs Dada did not really need the wheelchair, she wanted to have it changed. It was hitting the 10-year mark anyway. Wasn't 10 years the standard usage period for vehicles? She wondered why people made such a big deal out of it. Daniel was miffed about the predicament of his car too. He'd been trying to sell his beat-up Mazda for some time now, but there were no takers. Even Keng Boon, the old clerk who was usually contented and placid, had been so worried about his ageing car that he had to take a leave of absence. He reappeared a week later with a fresh haircut and brown-dyed hair as though his recently-bought Picanto had given him a new lease of life.

The expiring COE was haunting the men who shuddered to think about their cars becoming valueless when they hit the 10-year mark. It seemed to Cheryl Dada that a pandemic called Time (whose catchline went something like, "No time already lah!" or "Still got time meh?") had spread throughout the nation, and the men were wearing mechanical watches in their minds while the women had biological clocks sewn onto their wombs to avert the First World phenomenon known as depopulation or, to use the term Clare had taught her, voluntary childlessness.

Mrs Dada stared at the watch on her wrist. It looked like it belonged to a man. She did not understand cars and the other things that made men happy, but she assumed that an opportunity to buy a new car would be welcomed by most people. A decade seemed like a reasonably long time, long enough to collect substantial dents and dirt, so why did people not jump at the opportunity to change their cars? How long were they intending to keep their rides for—until the bumpers fell off? Anyway, when things get old they ought to be scrapped, she thought, running her eyes over the rusty silver on the rims of her wheelchair. And after all, 10 was the number of perfection, of an entire cycle, of... Of what? Mrs Dada could not remember.

Then the words sounded like thunder in her mind: "Ten is order." But who said that? "Ten is the number of the law." Was it Moses or Elijah? Cheryl Dada could see the rows of pews: 10 on each side of the room. They drew her eyes to the rugged cross that was nailed to the front wall.

There behind the pulpit she saw him. "Ten is order," he bellowed; the floor was vibrating. "Keep all ten, fail not one, my child," he bellowed again, his hazel eyes stared into hers. The man must be Jesus. Except he was Chinese. His yellow arms were outstretched: one hand clutching the Bible and the other held cartoon tracts. No obvious scars, Cheryl noted, squinting to see his palms. As for the wound on his side, her natural eyes could not see through his polo shirt.

Cheryl Dada stared hard into the vista, trying to summon the memory of the Chinese Jew. All this time she was sweating profusely, her clammy hands fiddling with the ends of her shirt. The little of the man she could remember melded with the face that emerged from the driveway.

"Good morning, Madam!" said Juwel high-spiritedly. He was walking briskly towards the bougainvillea that were potted by the porch and stopped in his tracks with his hands full of weeds when he saw her.

"Hello, Juwel," said Cheryl Dada, relieved to be interrupted.

"Madam eat already?" he asked politely.

"Not yet. Have you?" she said.

He nodded. "Yes, Madam. Today is rice and chicken curry."

Cheryl Dada gave a weak smile. For his sake, she hoped the curry wasn't sour.

"Wait ah, Madam," said Juwel. He went to the rubbish bin to throw the weeds in his hands and came back to her smiling sheepishly, as though her standing alone on the porch was his fault.

"Madam?" His voice quavered for a moment.

Sensing his apprehension, Cheryl Dada let her eyes wander behind him.

"I want to tell you something," he said.

What is it? she thought, glancing down at her watch.

"Madam, it is tonight. I cannot go to your party tonight," said Juwel, nodding apologetically, fingering the rusty trowel in his tool belt.

Her lips puckered, forming the silent surprise.

"I'm very sorry, Madam. Sorry."

Why? She almost asked.

I really want to, thought Juwel. The food is good and MC members will give out ang pows. And also Madam and Mr Dada are good people. Madam always gives him Brand's essence of chicken and Mr Dada would occasionally give him his old checked shirts. Juwel did not want to disappoint them. But it was his turn to wash the cars tonight. He had already asked Rajeet to cover two nights for him last month. Rajeet had his own commitments: two multi-storey car parks on Avenue 6 and a full-time job at the pest control company; and Juwel could not afford to skip nights this month. No work meant no money. He could not just work 44 hours a week in the nursing home; $560 was not enough. Back in Chittagong he could work forever, however long he wanted; there were no regulated labour hours. But here work stopped at six. All those extra hours spent in his dorm—how much did that cost him? He tried to work out the sum in his head: if he washed eight cars in four hours and each wash was five-dollars, he would earn about $40 a night, minus water money and soap money. But it was difficult to keep track of the money that was coming in because some nights he washed six cars and some nights there were no cars to wash.

Juwel was certain of one thing: the more hours he worked, the more money he made. Man-hours meant more men, more work, more money. July was a good month because he was washing almost every day. June, however, was not so good because many people went on holiday. Also, early in the month he had lost one packet of soap and had to ration the remaining bars by chopping them into tiny bits.

He wanted to tell somebody about the unease he felt for reusing the soap water and how his heart beat so quickly every time a police car drove by. But Mrs Dada would not understand. Why would Madam care? What seemed right to him was illegal to her. She was from a different world and he did not belong to her party.

"Very sorry, Madam, sorry I cannot go."

"It's all right," Cheryl Dada said after consideration. "I'll see you tomorrow."

"Yes, Madam," Juwel rushed on. "Sorry, Madam."

Watching Juwel turn away, Cheryl Dada found herself unwilling to let him go. She was sorry that he could not be there. He works too hard, she thought. He also seemed to be getting thinner—or was the green and red checked shirt too big for him? With an impulse to hold him, a maternal compassion welling up, she called out, "I'll ask them to keep some food for you!"

What a boy. With that sweet disposition and politeness, he can't be older than 25, she thought. Where had he learned all that gardening skills? From his father? Grandfather? Great-grandfather? (She heard that they married young—women as young as 12.) It always puzzled her how migrant workers like Juwel arrived here and seemed to know how to do the things they did. Like where did they learn to build something like Marina Bay Sands or the Star Vista? And the Esplanade? They must have had some training before they got here. Surely, not everyone could do it. Surely it wasn't as simple as following a building plan. There was nothing simple about filling up a rooftop infinity pool. The foreign workers did a good job—they were Chinese, right? Cheryl Dada recalled some dispute over wages on the news. Only the Chinese would dare to complain about unpaid wages and illegal deductions, only they would rally outside MOM and demand to be heard because they knew their rights.

Cheryl wondered if Juwel could build a pool too, and her eyes glittered at the thought of having a jacuzzi in the home. She was very pleased with the gardener, so much so that she might even miss him when it was his turn to receive the five-year long service award, which was a round-trip ticket to his home country. The blossoming pink bougainvillea that brightened the courtyard testified to his capabilities.

With his tool belt and gardening apron, Juwel certainly looked the part. His boots were caked in mud from grubbing about in the soil for diseased roots. The darkskinned, lanky boy carried with him the smell of dampened earth. Cheryl Dada took long and deep breaths, relishing the telluric scent that was still wafting in the air.

Only for a brief moment she thought of St Joan's. She closed her eyes and traced the uneven canopy of rain trees and the square field that took refuge under the viridescent dome.

(Juwel turned back to look at her. Something in Madam's tense face relaxed and softened, and she looked happier. Her face was very peaceful; it had a clarity that would make a good identity card photo. Juwel remembered how he had to use up half a bottle of gel to tame his curls so they would not fall to the front and cover his eyes. The immigration officer behind the camera was not nice at all—talking to him in a snarky tone. He was also thinking of how Madam's calm expression would befit an obituary picture; the kind that made the deceased look so at peace with death that living was passé and heaven was a real thing. The kind that turned mourning into jealousy.

Looking at her, affected by the feminine grace, Juwel forgot she was Madam from block A. In that moment, as his watch beeped twice, he saw his Ma again. The countenance roiled feelings of grief and shame. He began to tear up. It brought him back to that September, that weekend before he had left Chittagong. It all happened so fast: the application; the contract; the recruitment fees; the IPA and work permit processing; the visa and passport checks; Ma's death; the funeral; his departure.

Juwel was with his agent in Dhaka when he received the news. He flew back immediately on his agent's tab, just in time to see Ma before she was wrapped in the kafan. He did not recognise the pale-faced woman in a white dress; she looked like a teenager. Nani's hands were bright red from all the washing and cleaning. The same hands pulled the linen over the body and tied the sheets with ropes.

Outside the mosque, it was quiet. Nobody spoke a word, as though they did not know each other. Hands were raised and folded; the women behind were sniffling like they had colds. Once or twice there would be a roar: "Allahu Akbar"; then it was silent again. Then the truck started; its engine throbbed. Inside, where the body was loaded, it was quiet. The road was empty for a Friday afternoon. There was no sign of the usual stray dogs that scavenged for food by the wayside.

The cemetery was peaceful as expected. There were no birds chirping or frogs croaking. Only the sound of feet dragging across the grass. As shovels of soil heaped over the body, Juwel recited a prayer and said salam in his heart. He hoped that Ma's faith would take her to Paradise, someplace prettier than the overgrown burial site; he hoped there would be lilies and roses, birds and small animals, laughter.

Nani was waiting by the gate when it was over. Her arms reached out to Juwel and pulled him close; her face on his chest. He was afraid that Nani would hear his heart moaning when he was not supposed to cry. But she let him go without saying anything.

The crowd left as they had come, wordless and without tears. It was the quietest day of his life. Juwel left the next day for Dhaka. He flew to Singapore on Sunday and started work on Monday.)

Mrs Dada was thinking of St Joan's. The white and blue building was most pretty in the rain. Amidst the sound of pattering rain, she could hear the recess bell chiming; her watch beeping—and it was noon. She would go out to where the field met the trees and sweep her feet through the mounds of leaves and long black pods. The sounds of crisp leaves shuffling and twigs snapping, joined by the chatters of mynahs and crows—occasionally interrupted by the boys screaming in the neighbouring football field— woke the sleeping giant from its reverie. In moments like this saturated with the smell of soil and dried leaves, St Joan's slipped into Cheryl Dada's thoughts.

(Her eyes were resolutely shut, as though determined to block out the light. Madam must hate the sun, Juwel supposed, tracing the arches of her eyebrows. What was she thinking? The party tonight? He took a few steps closer, heedful not to alarm the woman, and allowed his eyes to rest longer on her fine face. The lines near her eyes were most distinct; they relaxed her worried face. Madam is pretty but she's getting old, he thought. Definitely older than Ma was. Juwel did not know if it was the stale curry or the thought of his mother's mummified body that roused in him an urge to puke. He dropped his tool belt and ran to the toilet.)

IF IT WERE UP TO MRS DADA

Cheryl Dada had forgotten most of St Joan's. She could not recall what the school building looked like, for it had been closed and torn down many years ago. The motto—*Steadfast in Duty*—was embossed on the school badge that was mostly white and blue with small flowers. She could piece together bits and bobs: the drink stall sold Sinalco and ice cream soda; a bowl of yellow noodles was 30 cents; the building did not have lifts; on the ground floor was a makeshift dental clinic operated by a masked couple. With the demolition it was as if St Joan's and its people had never existed. As if she were never there, as if nothing had happened.

A few years ago a co-ed school was built on the same plot of land. The paint was brighter, the building taller, the field trimmed. The canteen remained where it was; near the back gate. Cheryl passed by once when she was on home leave. There were boys and girls in green and yellow uniforms carrying their oversized bags, some holding hands, some buying ice cream from the Wall's cart by the traffic light. The older kids were hanging around the bus stop, waiting for the feeder bus; the younger ones stood by the side gate and looked out for their maids. Cheryl was standing there by the green fence where she had stood decades ago, looking into the football field; but everything was unfamiliar. She could no longer put the place to her memory. St Joan's was a disembodied fragment of the past. Cheryl wondered if she had imagined that year in school.

The one thing that assured her—what she remembered most vividly of St Joan's—was the perfume of the good damp earth with a hint of citrus. It flushed her with the hope of youth and brought her to the top of the world and to the end of herself. When the soil was roiled and the grass freshly cut, and her body suffused with warmth and midday languor, Cheryl Dada was reminded that the world was larger than the home.

But why was she thinking of St Joan's now? Where did the thoughts about it come from, all of a sudden? Her mind had no room for St Joan's, for the party was her priority. Today, the party was her world.

II

The clank of the iron gate swinging open brought Mrs Dada back to the present. Too open, she thought, watching closely as the gate slid across the concrete road, letting out a soft screech that was quickly devoured by the roar of the car engine. Mrs Dada stared hard at the passing Camry. She scrutinised the darkened window to see who was in the driver's seat, only to discover a blotchy likeness of herself in the glass that was formless and somewhat feral.

The car steered to the right of the car park—Mrs Dada peered again—and drove towards the back of the building. Did no one else notice? Had they forgotten about the escapes last year? Surely security must be tighter! What the hell was Cheok doing—sleeping again?

"Excuse me!" Mrs Dada cried out, following behind with her hand raised in the air, flagging the car down.

"Stop there," she shouted.

"I said stop," she yelled at the mysterious driver. But the car had disappeared from view.

"Lulu! Who was that?" Mrs Dada shouted, stepping back up to the porch, exhausted and riled, catching her breath.

"Can you hear me?" she cried out again, looking for Lulu who had disappeared into the following tables.

"I said the gate is too open!" Cheryl Dada yelled again, flapping her hands like the wings of a gigantic moth. "Damn it! It's too open!"

Lulu was busy laying the tablecloths. Her arms shuffled from left to right, right to left, smoothing out the creases that formed waves over the tabletop. She was already done with 20 tables. Catching sight of her red fingers, Lulu wondered if she would be able to wash the stain off later. ("Lulu!" Mrs Dada called out from behind.) Management should have acquired better tablecloths, she said rather begrudgingly. What a bunch of cheapskates. These ones were bloody lousy, the red colour running all over her hands! The stains on the nails are the hardest to remove, she lamented, examining her poorly manicured hands.

Eight more tables to go, Lulu told herself. She heard the screech of the car and was worried that the caterer had arrived early. It was only noon; she wasn't ready. She still had to sweep the floor and lay the cutlery. And she had to lay the candles for the table decorations. Lulu had got up at six this morning to run errands for the party, gone to the market and collected the stuff for the tables from the storage room. She had done so much but there was still more to do.

It's going to be a long afternoon, Lulu thought, looking at the chairs that were stacked up by the wall. They were like the rest of her days piling up, one after another; she was at the bottommost, bearing the responsibilities of the festivities ahead: Deepavali, Hari Raya Haji, the two remaining

Family Weekends, Christmas, the New Year... She could not wait for today to be over, for the year to be over.

The sound of the engine had stopped. Lulu waited to hear footsteps but it was quiet. It's no one important, she thought, and grabbed another tablecloth from the bag on the floor.

The car was gone, but Mrs Dada was still furious. Her privacy—this was her house!—had been invaded; worse still, nobody cared. Nobody was looking out for anyone here. "Where is everybody?" Mrs Dada found herself asking in a panic. The lack of security was troubling. There had been a rumour about someone escaping but Management refused to disclose any information. Of the money they have been pumping into the home, Cheryl thought, more should be spent on hiring competent people to guard the home. Nobody seemed to be uptight about their safety. Did no one care—Juwel? Cheok? Lulu? Daniel? Only she bothered enough to take down the car plate number.

People should care more, thought Mrs Dada, pacing the porch; her eyes were drawn to the mission statement written in red across the wall behind her: "To provide holistic quality care and round-the-clock concern with love for the elderly and needy," she mumbled, and wondered for a moment if the policy of care were the same as the provision of care. She hoped to God that all staff members would honour the promise and provide that holistic quality care tonight, for she had been looking forward to this evening. It was all she thought about for the past two months. But now that it was finally August, her mind kept slipping away to the littlest things like the bump left on her upper ear from the helix piercing she had got on her 35th birthday.

That was most definitely a midlife crisis, she reflected quietly, heaving a sigh. Just the other day she overheard Siew Eng and Felicia talking in the TV room about how single women above 35 were eligible to get a flat of their own. They could apply for BTOs or buy resale flats with bigger kitchens. There were also a few grants available but none for Siew Eng, who wanted to live near her parents. (What kind of grants, for instance? Some proximity grant; Cheryl Dada could not hear the rest of the explanation.) Siew Eng went on about how she would have tried for a BTO in the area if she were entitled to the $10,000 grant, for location was very important to her; Ang Mo Kio was very important to her. The irony of the whole housing situation was that Siew Eng and her parents were all living in Ang Mo Kio. She was just a street away from them.

From the porch facing the entrance, Mrs Dada fixed her eyes on the two BTOs across the road: one was white with orange stripes, the other was beige and green and taller. Both were also partly red because the flag buntings were up. A couple of flags over the parapet were hanging upside down.

The blocks of new flats were slim and high, not like the old ones. Certainly nothing like the house Cheryl grew up in. She remembered the tattered black sofa and boxy television that was at least three times more cumbersome than the one currently in the TV room. Very squarish, not rectangular or flat screen at all. It was the centrepiece of the living room that had cream-painted walls and was sparsely furnished.

Cheryl Dada let her mind linger on the memory of her old house and saw again the kitchen that was L-shaped, and the big silver basin. Underneath it was a metal square with a handle that had opened to the rubbish chute. She thought it was odd how all the units in the flat were connected by something so filthy and malodorous. Sometimes, when she opened the lid, she wondered if her neighbour who was also throwing stuff would be able to hear her if she said hello. The dark, hollow space was really echoic and sound travelled well through air. A hello can go a long way, Cheryl thought. All the way up to level 12 and down to level two.

Her fascination with the chute was short-lived. In a matter of months Cheryl began to avoid it, for the stench was intolerable when she opened the silver lid and she hated cockroaches. Once she pulled it open and an army of cockroaches climbed out. Afterwards it was impossible to get her to open the chute. She never again went near the sink.

What stupid architects, thought Cheryl Dada. Who in their right minds would think it was a good idea to bring the rubbish chute into the house? Was it not common sense— how could they not know that it was a gateway to roaches and rats and—God forbid!—snakes? The spawn of Satan! She had seen on the news that a python had climbed up the sewage pipe and hid in a toilet bowl. Hadn't there also been a python sighting in the industrial park last year? Cheryl Dada was easily and too often bedevilled by limbless vermin.

Thankfully, for the sake of hygiene and her peace of mind, the bin was outside now. Neither did she have to worry about rubbish or cockroaches because the cleaning lady emptied her bin twice a day.

Her mind ebbed and flowed over the BTOs with multi-storey car parks and electronic parking gantries. Indeed, the new flats had extra facilities and features that the old ones did not, but the space-efficient upgrades—for instance, a narrow gas pipe replaced the bulky gas cylinders—did not increase the actual living space. In fact, the flats had shrunk. Rectangular living rooms and bedrooms were reduced to squares. There was not enough space in the toilet for a bathtub, not enough space in the kitchen for a built-in oven. But most distressing to Cheryl was the tiny balcony. The balcony was where she had kept her tortoise tank, where her mother had played mahjong. Her grandmother had flipped thousands of love letters over the charcoal stove set up in the balcony of block 316.

According to Lulu, who had heard from her friend, the new balconies were not roomy at all: a small space in which to fit a washing machine and dry laundry. Lulu added that the current four-room flats also did not have a good-sized dining area.

Someone said, "How small? Can put table?"

"Don't think so lah."

"Aiyo just buy a small one—"

"Or the foldable type. Also can use mahjong table."

"Mai siao lah. Dirty how?"

"Kitchen got space?"

"No space then eat in the room lor."

"I also want to eat in the room."

"I also!"

"Kan ni na. You all siao ah?"

To that end Lulu interrupted: "People still eat in the dining area lah. My friend's employer ah, knock down the kitchen wall to make the dining room bigger. Only thing is, like that ah, less space for the kitchen. So small—like the security post like that."

Minutes later, as it might happen, the conversation went beyond the obelisk wall of the kitchen and became about some prudish neighbour and what was for lunch later. But the image of a kitchen as small as Cheok's room stuck with Cheryl Dada.

No, she remembered thinking then that she did not prefer the new flats. No, she would not want a house like that. So what if they look neater and have lifts that stop at every floor? she thought, and paused to recall those days when the highest the lift could go was up to the 11th floor.

Block 316 was 12 storeys high and splashed with colours. Colours of the rainbow, to be specific, Cheryl Dada thought, crossing her arms. Eyes still fixed on the flats, she felt a surge of triumph. The BTO flats did not have stone tables with chequers boards carved on them or mama shops or barbers in the void decks. No coffeeshops either. One of the flats across the road had a 7-Eleven and a cash machine, and that was about it. There was also a sandless playground that made no sense to her. The spongy carpet-like ground was awful—it reminded her of the mats in the toilets. Those always left her feet sticky. No, Cheryl Dada would rather live in block 316.

As soon as she thought about block 316, her mind floated to her mother with her in the house, just the two of them in unit #04-215. She shuddered. Between her mother's place and the BTO flats, it was still better to be here, Cheryl Dada concluded, looking at the concrete driveway, at Lulu pulling at the tablecloths, at the landscaped vista right outside the gate.

But if she could afford a house, things would be different, she thought, turning to look at the edifice behind her. It was white with blue window frames. The wooden porch beneath her feet extended into the common sitting area that was in the main building proper. The pale interior walls were not as white and immaculate as the outside (but they were next on the building improvement plan). Today the cedar chairs and benches, weathered to a silver grey, were unoccupied.

Cheryl wondered about the whereabouts of everyone, and turned around. The iron gate had recently been painted white; the previous coat was deemed too dark and unwelcoming. Management said it was "moody" and "unfriendly", as if metal could ever be unsteely. If it were not for the gates and the foxtail palms that flanked the entrance, the whole place would have had a white-picket-fence look.

Or a beach cottage. It was a very pretty-looking house. The façade was one of the reasons for Cheryl Dada's final decision to move out of her abode and she seldom regretted her choice. Many of the women had chosen the home for its appearance too. It also had a good track record—only three reported falls in the past year.

But having a house at 35, the thought came back to Cheryl Dada, that was different. Just think about that—her own house! Sure, it was not freehold and 99 years would eventually run out, but she wasn't going to live forever either. To have a house of her own for 99 years, that seemed more than enough.

If buying a house were possible back then, Cheryl Dada might be one of those people behind the grills, looking out the tiny windows at this beautiful white and blue house across the road. If living alone were a viable option, she might not be here, on the porch, under this fucking hot sun. Where would she be—London? Or Australia—her unmarried uncle had a farm in Perth. She could also go back to Melaka. So many possible places, so many untrodden paths. Yet here she was, this August afternoon, standing on the wooden porch, a home on a cul-de-sac, somewhere in Ang Mo Kio.

She could have explored more. All the if-onlys and what-ifs circling in her mind did not have to be hypothetical. Cheryl Dada might not have made the decisions she had at 35, many of which she regretted quite instantly, including the helix piercing. A house at 35, she pondered, rubbing the bump on her ear. How many more scars, unsightly keloids before one makes the right cut, the right decision?

The sound of bells chiming to the tune of "She Loves You" broke her concentration. She looked at her watch but the hour was not yet. It was 12.25.

"There's a call for you," hollered Lulu, as she walked over and passed the vibrating phone to Mrs Dada, who handled the device with an inspector's care. She placed her right thumb over the front camera and covered the lens on the back with her other hand.

"Hello?" The face on the screen twitched.

"Hello?" she echoed.

"Can you hear me?" the voice carried on in a rising tone; the face was frozen at 00:06. The number confirmed her suspicion. Somebody was listening. Something sinister, something evil! She had suspected for a long time that the millennium bug was still crawling. It made no sense that the devil would give up technology in the technological age. The Prophet Daniel had warned that knowledge shall be increased in the time of the end, and never has knowledge been deeper and more discovered that it is in present times. These are truly the last days, Cheryl avowed; her case was proving true. Never mind the naysayers. They said the Y2K bug had left, but it was worming elsewhere, burrowing escape tunnels in unknown computer systems. They said it would rain fire and brimstone; Cheryl Dada believed it would be an implosion because the devil was within.

"No!" she cried suddenly, and cried again, "No, no!" She would not let herself be one of those left behind. Never! Especially not today!

"No! Get away from me!" Cheryl swore vehemently. "Get the fuck away!"

But wait a minute, what were those two bloody stripes? Those thick red squiggly lines! It suddenly dawned on her that the face was a disguise. The red lips, the red lips were morphing and revealing their true selves. Worms! Beneath the blurry face were worms! The worms had one voice like Legion in the Book of Luke. It had found her. It was talking to her.

"Hello?" Legion wriggled. The numbers on the screen read 00:36.

The devil thought he could fool her but, oh no, she was smarter than that. No Legion was going to get her.

"No, no, no!" she shouted back at the legless creatures.

00:46. The devil's incarnation! It was clear to her that the worms had morphed into a two-headed serpent that was trying to crawl out of the glass. There was no doubt; it was coming for her.

"Not today!" Cheryl Dada screamed, holding the devious face away from her. Where was the crusher of the serpent's head? Nowhere near and present. She was on her own; the battle was at hand.

"Go away!" The beast must leave. "In the name of Almighty Lord! I cast thee out!"

Cheryl Dada slapped the face once, twice, thrice. She went at it harder, more zealously, yelling again, "I cast thee out!"

Suddenly the face on the glass rippled and contorted, like raging waters in a storm. The sea split and out of its mouth erupted: "Mum! For God's sake—"

Then it was silent. The screen froze again. It was 01:16. Satan's number again. Cheryl was sure it was the devil on the line. The devil was trying to play nice, but she was no Eve. Communication in low resolution is extra trippy. Cheryl Dada flung the device out of her hand; it landed on the concrete floor. She heard a crack. The serpent was gone.

Lulu, who was wiping the tables at that time, lifted her head and saw the phone flying across the driveway. Her eyes followed its shimmery trail as it glided under one of the tables and landed on its screen beside her bare brown feet.

"Oh, for the love of Christ!" Lulu muttered under her breath. Does she know the price of one of these? It's the third time this year. If she didn't want to talk to Madam Clare, she could have just hung up. What story to tell Mr Dada this time? That the phone dropped into the toilet bowl? She was running out of excuses to cover up for her charge. Or she could just tell the truth. But no, she could not bear the sight of Mr Dada's pitiful face. The man has already been through so much, she thought. Did Madam deserve his goodness? Lulu did not want to judge. She only knew that rich people like Madam were a disgrace and she couldn't care less about their problems.

Lulu had concluded that rich people were brats. She knew this before she had come to Singapore. Her first employers—an American couple from New Bedford living in Hong Kong—put her in charge of their twin boys, Spencer and Jake. The brothers' favourite game was fetch. They had no dog, so they threw the ball and Lulu fetched.

The game was eventually banned in the house when the ball broke the family's prized cloisonné vase. The boys blamed it on their helper's poor fetching skills and she was dismissed the next month. She bottled up the injustice and applied for another job.

The next stint brought Luisa Mae Morales to Singapore. Her employer was a French–Chinese couple with an adopted 16-year-old girl. They were very messy people who lived in a big mansion. But cleaning was the least of Lulu's problems.

The beautiful Angelique Marie Yang-Dumont was a kleptomaniac. She stole from her parents' drawers and took coins from Lulu's money tin. This went on for months. Lulu knew better than to tell on her. But when she came back to her room one day to find her stack of $10 notes gone, Lulu knew she had no choice. It was one thing to take a handful of coins, another to take hundreds. Thus it was time to not play nice and confront the thief. Lulu knew that her word would not stand against the face of an angel: hers was regarded as a poor brown face; Angelique Marie had big blue eyes. Since flight was no longer a choice, Lulu decided to fight shrewdly. If Justice had arms, they were her own.

Part of the plan was to creep into the young mistress's room and take back the loot. What's stolen cannot be more stolen than it already is, she reasoned with herself. Anyway one cannot be more wrong than one was wrong—was it called the law of double jeopardy? She learned from *Law and Order*, the Yang-Dumonts' favourite series, that one cannot be charged for the same crime twice. That would be a miscarriage of justice. So, with a peace of mind—and Mother Mary's blessings, hopefully—Lulu went into the room when the family was in Nice for Christmas and took everything.

To say the young mistress was furious was a gross understatement. Her anger was doubly squared because she could not expose Lulu without implicating her own proclivity for theft, so she wailed and cursed words Lulu had never heard before. The spew must have been offensive—one did not have to be French to know that—but the sing-song quality of the language softened the edges of each syllabus—"*Ce n'est pas ma faute. C'est injuste! Fait chier! Putain cet enfoiré je t'en merde. Sale connard de merde! C'est vraiment des conneries! Va te faire foutre! Va te faire enculer!*"—and the entire tirade reached Lulu's ears like the sound of waves gently breaking on the Cebuano coast.

Lulu resigned a month later. Because she had only worked for one year, Lulu asked for a refund of the agent fees for the second year that she did not serve. She brought all of the money home, including Angelique's loot, and stayed in Manila with her in-laws for a while. She got pregnant and had a baby, and then her husband fell very ill. At around that time, the agent called and told her about the opening in Mrs Dada's home—which was a healthcare assistant job, encompassing a range of responsibilities from offering residents help with their day-to-day life tasks to assisting with the home's community building. Baby

Magdalene and Kenneth needed her, but Lulu knew what they really needed was money. So she left for Singapore when Magdalene was three months old.

Lulu's past work experience had determined for her that rich children were spoilt because their parents were spoilt first. With time passing, and their parents dying, they might sober up. Lulu could pardon rich kids, but rich old people had no excuse. Didn't wisdom come with age? Madam's 51 already and she also looks wise, Lulu thought, but why does she act like a child? It was true that Cheryl Dada was regressing, her body mass shrinking; she was losing bone density, chugging Ensure every morning. Still, Lulu thought, wrinkles and grey hair must indicate maturity, and at the very least translate to some thought and sense. But Madam is not sensible, Madam is a child, Lulu vouched again, glancing over at the woman who was staring vacantly at the nearby flats.

How calm she seemed, almost serene. It was hard to imagine that this was the same obnoxious woman who had flipped over the bowl of ah balling on the dining table yesterday because Mr Song had overlooked her dislike for peanuts. She went on and on about how the head cook was wielding his frying slice like Moses's staff and should be fired for his negligence. If only Madam could see that in his eyes she was just another crazy woman, a difficult resident, a part of the job.

Lulu understood that people hurt other people because they themselves had been hurt. She knew all that theory on circles: karma, vicious cycles, chasing tails, turning tables, what goes around comes around. Everyone has a sob story—rich people included, though they might be too proud to tell it. Pride erected a brick wall between her and them. Though she saw through the old ladies and their antics, and as much as she wanted to sympathise, Lulu could not halt the great partition forming within: her feelings were split between sympathy and aversion; her loyalty was torn between God and self.

The edge of the red and white checked cloth slipped and Lulu pulled it back into place, tying it to the leg of the table. Squatting down, she heard her stomach rumble. It must be almost one. The tablecloths were taking too much of her time. She had to hurry; she still needed to iron Mrs Dada's dress for the party. She mumbled something inaudible and rubbed her stomach.

Mrs Dada watched Lulu as her eyebrows knitted together into a slight frown. She studied her expression and could not decipher it—the slight elevation and furrows, the thick lips pressed tightly. She understood only that it was an expression that was often seen on the faces of the healthcare staff who were from a class and country that she was excluded from. What was Lulu thinking of? Was she missing her family? Her daughter must be about two now. What's her name again—Mary? It might have been another name in the New Testament.

Poor Lulu, Mrs Dada thought, suddenly empathetic. She must be beating herself up for leaving her baby girl, without her mother, in the hands of a divine power. The crucifix she wore—that must be for her family's protection. The other nurses said her husband had terminal lung cancer even though he had never smoked a cigarette. Lulu never confirmed the rumour; she never mentioned anything like that. No one knew his health status or even if he were still around.

Mrs Dada wondered about the little girl, a child alone in a Third World country. That can't be good, she thought, as she envisaged a dark-haired girl in a pink dress with the talking Elmo Lulu had bought from the charity flea market last year. Mrs Dada tried to think of better scenarios: of little Mary in a sandy playground with ice cream smeared all over her cheeks, of her tying her shoelaces on her first day of kindergarten, of her playing hopscotch and rubbing off the chalk lines on the floor. Was she the Barbie kind of girl or Cabbage Patch kid? Hot Wheels or Lego? Maybe she liked to read in the library.

But her mind kept drifting to another scene: the little girl in her pink dress, which had become shredded and ash-ridden, standing in the middle of a grey ruined city with wrecked buildings and rubble surrounding her, with no father in sight, no Lulu beside her. Despite her good intentions, Mrs Dada was looking at the outside world, at Lulu and little Mary's world, through an opaque and sturdy lens that, framed and painted with privilege, could neither be polished nor broken by its wearer. Behind the invisible glass, a tear was forming in her eye.

III

Cheryl Dada was half-yawning when Vikash came up to her.

"Good afternoon, Madam Cheryl," he said enthusiastically, flashing a wide smile. His teeth were pristinely white.

"Hello, Vikash," said Cheryl Dada.

His hand was in his pocket, jangling the keys. "Madam, I going to collect fruits for the kitchen. For tonight dinner. Then after that I go pick up the day care clients."

"Oh," said Cheryl Dada, "I thought dessert is catered—"

"Yah, they suppose to do that," he said, keeping his poster-boy smile. "But the almond jelly too sweet. Then the fruit cocktail—the can type—Miss Lina say also cannot. She say too sweet for residents. So Mr Song and the kitchen going to do fruit salad."

"Ling Na," Cheryl Dada corrected him. Of course she would object to it, she thought to herself. That woman said no to tau sar piah, orh nee, tau suan, bubur char char, tau huay. Even chin chow with longan was not allowed. They were either too sweet or too cooling. "Cannot, cannot. This one not good for you," she nagged. "That one too much sugar." She kept repeating how bad the sweets were for them that even Poh Choo, the most forgetful of the women, was starting to remember that she had diabetes.

What a killjoy. Maybe because she was not from around here, Ling Na did not understand what these traditional desserts meant to them. Cheryl Dada's favourite dessert was chendol: partly because of the coconut milk, mostly because she remembered juicing pandan leaves and making those green slippery jellies with her grandmother. Ling Na's sugar-free desserts and fruits were very healthy but brought no pleasure and brought back no memories. Other approved desserts included a variety of unsweetened soups: peanut soup, ginger soup, green bean soup and sweet potato soup. Cheryl Dada did not like soups. They made her pee a lot in the night. Ling Na was the food police, and Cheryl did not like her one bit.

"Her name is Ling Na," Cheryl Dada repeated, looking at the young man to make sure that he got it.

"Yes, Madam," Vikash said, his jovial smile faded to an embarrassed grin. The Chinese names were the toughest to get right. They did not pronounce his name correctly either but that didn't matter to him. It was a language difference and Vikash knew it wasn't their fault.

"Miss Ling Na say..." Vikash paused to find on the old woman's face the permission to continue. He went on: "Miss Ling Na say the dessert cannot. So I going to get fruits. Mr Song want watermelon, oranges, pineapple and honeydew. Madam, you want anything? I can get for you."

Yes, Cheryl Dada was tempted to oblige. It was just like Mr Song to come up with such a boring fare. Watermelon and honeydew... What was he thinking? Tonight's a party, not a Chinese banquet! How about passion fruit for a change? Or pomegranates for antioxidants? Some New Zealand kiwis would be great as well. She could almost hear Daniel say, "No, that is too expensive." "No, we don't have the funds for that." And of course the market on Avenue 10 would not have passion fruit or anything exotic, so Vikash would have to make a stop at Cold Storage.

But there was no Cold Storage in Ang Mo Kio. That's for atas people, Cheryl thought, and conjured up images of Cold Storage in Great World City, Takashimaya, United Square, Cluny Court, Jelita—areas in which she had never resided and did not want to visit. Yet, isn't Ang Mo Kio atas enough? Isn't the "ang mo" in Ang Mo Kio the same as ang moh?

Cheryl organised Ang Mo Kio in her head. There was Avenue 1, where Bishan Park was; Avenue 2—that was where St Joan's used to be; Avenue 3 was the Ang Mo Kio Central area, and the street across was Avenue 8. The markets helped her to sort out Avenues 4, 9 and 10. Avenue 6 was easy to remember: it had a big mosque. Cheryl was not familiar with Avenue 5—she thought it was where the industrial buildings and factories were. And then there was Avenue 7; Avenue 7 was the home.

Ang Mo Kio was a huge area—possibly the biggest residential town in Singapore, also one of the oldest. Yet there was not a single Cold Storage. The best they got was the Hypermart—not even an NTUC Finest!—that carried Australian broccolis and SunGold kiwis.

Cheryl considered if she'd like some kiwis for tonight, but decided that the yellow flesh looking like vomit was not a good colour. The Hypermart served the Ang Mo Kians well. Cheryl liked it. Not forgetting that it supplied her favourite Aseel dates. These were not the run-of-the-mill variety but were the best of Sindh, organic and super fleshy, quite like the ones she had bought from Aabpara Market years ago. Cheryl couldn't remember the last time she visited Islamabad and what had brought her there in the first place, but the buttery sweetness of the dates stayed with her.

Should she ask Vikash to make a stop at NTUC? The dates were tempting. But no, that was not part of his job. Vikash is not a driver, Cheryl reminded herself. He is a HCA, she said silently, reading the badge that was clipped to his shirt. The letters arranged themselves in her mind: Health and Community Administration? Head of Community Activities? Vikash must be in charge of something to do with the community, but she could not say exactly what. She only knew he was not a driver.

Vikash, too, was confused about his job. He often thought of himself as a driver, though he wasn't part of FM. For he was most comfortable behind the wheels. He volunteered to collect the medical supplies; deliver documents; fetch people to and from the MRT station; bring Lucky to the vet; pump petrol at the Shell station that was two blocks away. These trips were like excursions around the city; they made him feel excited about being here. Going on the CTE, driving out of Ang Mo Kio, Vikash had this odd sense of space expanding. In the van, he could steer the direction of his life, he had control for those 20 or so minutes. He was, at the very least, moving. It was nice to be reminded that the world was more than this white and blue building in the heart of Ang Mo Kio. That life continued outside the home.

Keys bulged in his pocket; there was another bunch dangling from his belt. Those were the keys to his house in Vellore, all three were rustic and looked heavy. He kept them with him, just in case. Vikash was always on standby, even when he was not on duty.

He wasn't always like that: alert and ready. From the time he had applied for this job to waiting for his work permit to be approved, Vikash was mostly apprehensive. He thought the application would be rejected and he would instead move to Chennai or Kochi—he heard that they were building hotel boats there and more jobs were opening up. But his Appa was confident, especially since Dr Achari had promised to vouch for him. It did not seem to bother Appa that Vikash had no experience in healthcare. His brothers, Venkat and Vasu, were already in Delhi training to become experts in the construction industry even though they knew nothing about building. It was Vikash's turn: he was 18.

Appa believed that Vikash would have a better chance at life if he left India; Amma wanted him out of her sight after what he had done to his sister. Vikash had to leave, and Singapore was a door swung wide open.

When Venkat and Vasu said Singapore was a good place, they were telling Appa and Amma the truth. Yes, there was more money to earn. There was always work to do: new roads to build and old roads to fix. They said it was multi-racial and inclusive, a land of opportunities. They reported that there were many Indians in Singapore and most of them did not speak Hindi, which was fine by them since they preferred to speak Tamil. There was a place called Little India where they could get a big bowl of koozh for about 80 rupees. They said the Chinese people had their own version that was really just rice and water and it was more expensive—at least 150 rupees. They said life was good in Singapore, though they couldn't wait to go home.

What Venkat and Vasu did not say—and what Vikash later found out for himself but also would not say—was how they had to work on the roads in the rain because not working on rainy days was counted as forced leave. They said they ate well, that the curry here was good; what they meant was the curry gravy made the dry rice more palatable. They said they had their own space; but they would not say that home was a makeshift dormitory made from a container block. They said it was quiet, much like their village back home; a place called Lim Chu Kang.

What Vikash could not see back there in India, and what he was beginning to see now after being here for six months, was that being truthful was not the same as telling the truth. Appa and Dr Achari seemed to have understood the principle of truth much earlier. Like when the agent called and asked for a certificate, Appa immediately went to consult with Dr Achari, who wrote back with a written account of the day Vikash had helped to attend to the patient who had a gash in her head from a road accident. Dr Achari was right to say that Vikash tried to stop the bleeding with his shirt and whatever cloth he could find, and even antisepticised the open wound. He added that Vikash performed CPR on the patient, compressing her chest with so much force that caused two fractured ribs. That shows dedication to save lives, explained the doctor. Even though he was not a certified nurse, Vikash responded quickly and appropriately in an emergency and demonstrated potential to be an outstanding healthcare assistant. Everything in the testimonial was true; Dr Achari told the truth of what happened that day.

But if it were up to Vikash, he would have told them that the patient was Vani. That he too was bleeding when he brought her in; that his hands were covered in both their blood when he pressed on her chest; that he had retched when they carried her away. But the agent did not need to know that.

Why should it matter how he got here? thought Cheryl Dada, looking at the man who was too young to be the Head of Community Activities. He did not need to explain himself; it did not matter to her how he became a HCA. Vikash was very hardworking and took the initiative to deliver stuff and drive people around. That was all that mattered.

"No, I don't need anything," said Cheryl Dada, as though to assure him.

"What?" said Vikash distractedly.

"I mean I don't want any fruits."

Vikash stared blankly at her. His arms down along the sides of his body stiffened as he remembered Vani's weightless body.

"I said it's okay. Don't buy anything for me," said Cheryl Dada, with patience. "You'd better go now, before the market closes."

"Yes, Madam. Yes, I go now," Vikash finally uttered, realising that she was concerned for him.

"Thank you, Madam," he said, stretching his smile, as the last of his words petered out, as he turned towards the iron gate.

Cheryl Dada was pleased with herself. She had paid enough attention to him to notice that he was not as happy as his smile. It was a professional front: the kind of smile one puts on in order to look casual and approachable, the kind that wipes away the sadness of being human. But one can only hold a smile for so long. After that it is just lip service. Smiles are too precious, she thought. Vikash should only smile when he's happy. Nobody should be obliged to smile. If he keeps smiling like that, he'll forget what it feels like to be truly happy. That boy has not been happy in a long time, thought Cheryl Dada, watching Vikash's silhouette slowly diminishing until it went into the van.

As Mrs Dada was thinking of teeth and lips and smiles, Lulu, who had finished setting the tables, sidled up to her.

"Time to—"

The beeping sound of the Casio watch startled them. Mrs Dada turned and was dismayed to see Lulu. Lulu glanced back at her, hoping she would understand that she did not mean to interrupt her; but Mrs Dada grimaced and looked away, refusing to turn off the hourly chime. The beeping went on.

The next few seconds they stood side by side in silence. Cheryl Dada looked fixedly at the two pigeons that were prancing on the road. Orangey feet, she noted; even the albino one has orange feet. It looked like a dove. She thought it might be a sign from God that tonight would be peaceful.

Lulu lowered her head. Her eyes focused on the medicine cup in her hand. The pills were white and clean. The Metformin looked like a regular Panadol. If only they made it smaller and more colourful, Lulu thought, perhaps it'd be easier to get Madam to take them.

Or if they made them sweet like cough syrup—like Pi Pa Gao, Cheryl Dada continued in her head. Better still if they came in the form of an energy drink that she could gulp down. Pharmaceutical science needs to be more creative and considerate, she thought.

In spite of the dissimilitude of minds, the scene was convivial, as if Mrs Dada and Lulu were discharged from the lives they had been living and were presently standing on the same path, tethered to the same mind. Cheryl Dada was 21 years older and Lulu was the woman who took care of her; but for the span of the moment they were equal; two women yoked together; differences levelled.

Their lives were shaped by the home, both in a moral and physical sense. There was an order that the women had to follow.

0630 to 0730—Shower and grooming
0730 to 0900—Breakfast
0900 to 1000—Morning exercise and OT/PT
1000 to 1100—TV
1100 to 1230—Lunch
1230 to 1430—Community activity (including but not limited to gardening, shopping at Ang Mo Kio Hub, still life painting, cooking demonstration and tasting, Chinese dance, ukulele class or pet-assisted therapy)
1430 to 1530—Tea and snack
1530 to 1630—Nap
1630 to 1730—Afternoon exercise and OT/PT
1730 to 1900—Dinner
1900 to 2000—TV
2000 to 2100—Supper
2100—Lights out

In a place where time was prescriptive, each hour written out like a blurb for a handbook titled *Resident Focused Care Plan* to ensure proper and healthy conduct, their inactivity was a quiet rebellion, a joint effort to switch things up, to loiter for a moment longer before following what was next on the schedule.

"Time to eat medicine," Lulu resumed. The last beep of the watch sounded. She stared at the plastic cup of white pills in her hand. It was in the way of lunch.

Cheryl heard nothing. A fly buzzing, she thought. Lulu's pleas were as unnecessary as the nuisance brown spots that popped up unannounced on her arms. She knew that to be nagged at was protective rather than punitive, but there was something in all that mollycoddling that irked her.

"Madam, eat your medicine," said Lulu, trying a gentler tone.

"No, thank you," said Mrs Dada.

"Madam, it's one o'clock already. Faster eat then can go for lunch," Lulu said, her smile waning. "Please, Madam. Later no more food ah. It's already past lunchtime."

"I will pass today," Mrs Dada answered, and shifted her attention to the flats on the other side of the road.

"Most of them are vitamins, Madam. Not bitter at all. They good for you."

Mrs Dada yawned.

Things were back to normal. It was as if they had not shared the passing moment. As if they never understood each other. What a nag, Mrs Dada thought. She wished for Lulu to go away.

"Madam, think of your bad leg and sore neck."

Mrs Dada was annoyed. Does she think I've forgotten?

"Okay, never mind," Lulu said, somewhat resignedly. On some level she pitied the woman for having to take so many pills at her age, but Lulu had her chores for the day to complete and she was at this moment famished. Her schedule for the afternoon depended on how persuadable Madam was.

"You know, no medicine, no food, right?"

"I'm not hungry."

"Don't be like that, Madam. If you don't have it, you will—"

Did she mean—? But do people—can it really be? Will I really die from a drug underdose? Mrs Dada wondered, slightly tickled. Was there such a thing—the opposite of an overdose? That'll be news: *Woman Dies from a Fatal Underdose.* Ha! Ha! What a quip. Just think about that—of all the ways to die, she dies from not having enough medicine. How unheroic. Better to fling herself out the window to be lifted by the air. *Woman Dies from Flying.* Now that would be an awesome headline—

Feeling bad about the words that slipped through her mind, Lulu turned away from her charge, and was willingly taken by the silvery sheen of the forks and spoons set neatly on the tables. Her eyes wandered involuntarily from one table to the next, following the trail of metals shimmering in the sun. That was her finished work, the work of her bare red-stained hands. All that squatting and bending over was sure to come back and bite her in old age. Or maybe tomorrow her muscles would start to ache. This was the kind of work she did at the home but it was not backbreaking work. Or foot stinking work. She remembered the skin on her father's legs was perpetually wrinkled from prolonged soaking in the field, the stench of rotting flesh that filled up the house when he took off his boots.

Lulu felt sick to her stomach. The people here knew no hardship; Madam certainly did not. This was probably the hardest her life had ever been and it was not nearly a fraction of what her parents had to go through. Life was unfair; there was no denying it, no way to sugar-coat it. The world had a ranking in place and she was way below. People like Angelique Marie and Madam were high up. Life was unfair; she had accepted it. But why was God unfair too? He had to know that it was most hard for her to be away from her baby. Please don't let it get any harder, Lulu prayed in silence, looking up to the sky.

Then, as if her God were real and listening, the thought of the 22,000 pesos that came in every month darted into her mind and Lulu broke into a smile. One day, she would have her own party with fancy silverware and tablecloths and candlelights. She and Magdalene would have the VIP table to themselves. They would be together again. Two more years, two more years, Lulu muttered to herself.

Thinking of the party, Lulu suddenly realised that she had leverage over the older woman. Every resident had her quirks and soft spots, even those fitted with nasogastric tubes had their preferred flavour of milk. One of Madam's many idiosyncrasies was her love for parties.

Lulu looked to Mrs Dada and said resolutely, "No medicine, no party." Confidence was brewing in her. She knew it was enough; she had won.

Mrs Dada caught the smirk on Lulu's face. She did not want to bow down, especially not now since Lulu had a hold on her and was delighting in the reversal of power. Cheryl Dada hated to give in more than she wanted to be given way to.

IF IT WERE UP TO MRS DADA

Certain that her charge would take the medicine, Lulu left the cup and a bottle of water on the porch and went inside. It was time for lunch—time to be alone.

Mrs Dada waited until she was sure that Lulu was gone. Finding herself on her own, no longer interrupted, she relaxed her tense body and carefully lowered herself until she was able to feel the ground. She took off her sandals and slowly pulled her legs under her. Her calf muscles were stiff; the spindly legs did not seem to belong to her.

Sitting down, the view was different. Mrs Dada looked around: the walls stared hues of white and yellow back at her; the concrete was grey and slightly glistening. Sunlight perforated the space and cast light on the little plastic cup that was sitting beside her. The doctor had prescribed those pills for six months now but she could not tell whether they had done her any good. She emptied the cup into her hand, put all seven pills in her mouth and swallowed some water.

The pills left a powdery trail in her mouth and the bitterness affected her taste buds. The instructions should have indicated to take them after food rather than before, because now that Cheryl had swallowed the pills, she had lost her appetite and felt more infirm than before.

Cheryl Dada associated medication with weakness. Her mother told her she had a weak immune system and that she needed to be stronger because they could not afford the doctor. Despite her will, Cheryl was prone to sickness, especially as a child. Her mother must have felt that in many ways she was a burden—Cheryl was draining her inheritance money and insensible for her age, always talking to her dolls and reading the same few books over and over again.

From the pleats of her memory came a particular August night back in block 316. It was one of those vivid memories of her weakest self; one of those nights that often arrived swiftly and without notice. There she was, sprawled on the bed, nauseous from shame. She thought if she could sleep, the pain would go away, but no length of sleep could restore the holiness that had guarded her heart, the holiness marred by her self-efforts to get right with her Heavenly Father.

Since secondary school—be it St Joan's or St Rita's, where she had been transferred to—Cheryl had been trying to be righteous: she was serving in the worship ministry; she was a regular in her cell group; she was about to enter university. She was doing everything right but she was never perfectly sure of her salvation, for she could not forget what had passed.

Yet what was she missing exactly? Why did she keep longing for what she could not have? Cheryl was tired of striving, tired of keeping her head high when all she wanted to do was to sleep and forget. She needed to rest; she needed a good long rest. She took one pill, and then two more. Then she gathered the remainder of her strength and held up the last pill to the lambent light. It was pristine, almost sparkling. Like the rest, it was so smooth it glided down her throat.

Cheryl waited for the medicine to take the pain away. Her mouth was dry and bitter, and her arms were heavy. The glass of water on the bedside table was untouched. The ice was melting, the water still cold. The knitted coaster underneath the glass was soaked. Cheryl wanted a sip, but the water was clean and sacred. She dared not take what she did not deserve. The water, pure and transparent, was watching her, silently judging her. Like the apparition who was sitting by the wardrobe with both knees pulled up against its chest and hands fastened to its vague body. Its back was glued to the wall—how long had the ghastly figure been there? It was inching backwards, retreating and shaking its head. But where was it going? Where could it possibly go? Behind was an impossible wall and it had already etched itself onto it.

Cheryl Dada mumbled a name that clarified the night. "Sarah," she said, and could not restrain a tinge of melancholy. A few times she repeated the name that stirred up in her a longing to hold fast to the face that was slowly vanishing; the face belonged to the figure that was scaling the wall of the room to get away from her only to reappear in the walls upon which her memory was built.

Everything was about Sarah. Like a birthmark, she was always already there. To know Cheryl was to know Sarah.

Cheryl Dada now saw her more clearly; the car park, the driveway, the round tables, the empty cup on the porch receded. The open space before her narrowed into a four-walled room. She saw Sarah there, and here, in the classroom on the second floor with the window overlooking the field. The exact year escaped her. It must have been around '77 or '78. The year the Carpenters released their greatest singles on cassette. Cheryl had this set in her mind because she had spent all her ang pow money on the tape to find out that "Only

Yesterday" was not the same as "Yesterday Once More". That was four dollars blown on the wrong compilation of songs. Though it was no one's fault, Cheryl secretly blamed the band. Her interest in them began to wane from then on. It was also about that time that Karen Carpenter began losing much of herself and stopped playing the drums.

So it was that year, one rainy morning, they met in Home Economics class. The teacher was demonstrating how to pare and segment an orange. Up until this moment—Mrs Something was removing the rind—Cheryl had not noticed the new student who was sitting beside her.

Details were coming back to her. The moment of realisation, of discovering the unfamiliar figure sitting beside her, was one of delight mixed with horror. Cheryl was enchanted by the girl yet genuinely frightened by her sudden appearance. Where had she come from? When did she come into class? The other students did not seem surprised by the new addition at all. The nonchalance made Cheryl wonder if she was imagining things again. Around this time, her mother told her that badly behaved children who sinned against God were punished with the curse of the third eye. With fear Cheryl became hypervigilant about her surroundings, checking at all times that she was not afflicted with the visual abnormality. For a while she hid Doraemon and her white rabbit away lest they were demonic. She kept her eyes to the floor in case she saw what she was not supposed to see. Thus when Cheryl beheld the curious face in class that day, she assumed its owner was unreal.

The boyish figure was hunched over the table, staring dreamily at the teacher. (Mrs Something was trimming the pith.) From where Cheryl was sitting, the new girl boasted a strong jawline that narrowed into a full and haughty chin. As she propped her head up on one elbow, her tousled hair, more brown than black, fell to the side and revealed a childish face. Her nose reminded Cheryl of a button mushroom. It twitched when she sniffed. The new girl was set apart from the neighbourhood kids at St Joan's—so how had she not noticed her earlier? Cheryl asked herself, as her gaze roved over the stranger who was stuffing stray wisps of hair behind her ear. She was outstanding, taller than most of them. The girl had a bronze tan that was unusual around here. Also, she was very lean, Cheryl noted. She would have been called sangpo, if not for the long and wiry arms that suggested that she played sports. Cheryl thought it was weird that her hands were darker than her face. Did she play basketball? But that was a boy's sport. Maybe it was netball.

The memory was clear but confusing. She had come to herself through Sarah; yet it was as if she had come to herself after passing out, in a state of delirious torpor, reaching for something that was describable only in terms of its absence. Things do not have to be verifiable, just veritable. Upon waking, what Cheryl felt was real, but reality was in its vaguest form. Without form, Sarah had no consistency; her very existence was carried by an eternal principle of confusion and absent-mindedness. Sarah was temperamental like that. Sometimes she was the villain, other times she cried victim, each image supplanting the other. It was as if Sarah preceded Sarah, and Cheryl did not know which version she preferred. Only even the worst version of Sarah was better than none of her.

It must have been nearly 40 years since the day they had met. The events of the day were escaping Cheryl Dada; flashes of the kitchen classroom slipped in and out of her mind. The air was now smelling like fresh orange. The little things of Sarah came rushing into the present, teasing her of better times, but would not stay long enough to take her back. When is the past ever enough for the present?

Why did she keep thinking, thinking? How did she get so good at thinking? Her mind could not stop; all that activity, that thinking turned her head grey. When she was younger she assumed it was Math that sucked the colour from her hair. Later in life she blamed it on precoital anxiety, prenatal stress, postnatal blues, post-postnatal blues. Now that she knew the real issue was her dramatic mind, next time she'd try feeling instead. She must stop thinking. Might as well, for soon it would become blur, as it always did when the effects of the seven pills kicked in.

Just then the watch struck two. It expelled the last vestige of Sarah from her memory. Cheryl Dada closed her eyes for a quick rest, though in the darkness she hungered for more to see. Then her mind was a blank. All she could hear was her heart pounding, more and more slowly, against the rhythm of the beeping watch.

IV

When she opened her eyes, the weather was still scorching. Mrs Dada remembered she was supposed to get the flowers. She had given up on the breeze and cool temperatures; also her light, airy top was not cooling at all. The sun was bent on burning this side of the island. Mrs Dada was beginning to see that she had no choice. Someone had to get the flowers, and since going to the Hub was no more an option and the sun was merciless, she might as well head to the garden now.

She put on her sandals, adjusted her chiffon top and slowly pulled herself up. She felt a little wobbly; her bad leg was acting up again. Maybe she should have listened to Clare and bought the walking cane after all. Cheryl Dada was starting to regret her decision. Some things were non-negotiable. Age was something that she could not fight; there was no use fighting the pain in her leg.

Arthritic fingers, swollen knee, gout, migraine—what was next? Hopefully death, she grumbled. Her arm reached for her knee and gave it a gentle rub. Not today, she beseeched her reluctant body.

She stiffened a little when she came to the edge of the porch, wondering which route she should take.

She considered going for lunch but decided she was not hungry. Also, the thought of bumping into Lulu in the hall was sickening. It was too soon to be reminded of her defeat.

Looking at the clear driveway, Mrs Dada contemplated her choices. The long way, which was her usual path, had been barricaded to make room for the guests' cars. She would have to go by way of the secondary route—a shortcut nonetheless—with less greenery and fewer squirrels. She did not mind it much, but for the dreadful slope.

Mrs Dada crossed from the porch to the driveway and walked parallel along the iron gate. As she walked, her fingers ran along the vertical bars, sounding a melodious *dong dong dong* that disrupted the quietude of the afternoon. Where was everybody? Where were the nursing and FM staff? Daniel said more people were put on duty today, but few were present. Lulu, she knew, was probably in the kitchen and Juwel was already gone. Daniel and Yu Yu were also not in sight. They were the most sensible ones, the heads of their departments, yet they too were missing.

Maybe they aren't going to come tonight, she thought. They must have hated her for all her demands and extra requests. But it was important to her that the chairs had cushions on them; the wooden chairs were too hard to sit for long. The guests must be most comfortable tonight, she thought. As for the candles, they were necessary to light up the venue—those sharp white fluorescent lights were awful! She could not bear those void deck lights. She must have her vanilla-scented tea lights!

So it was a specific list, Cheryl admitted to herself, kicking the pebble that was in her way. What was wrong with wanting starry napkins and some flowers for the tables? The theme was red and white, stars and the moon—did they not get the memo? Tonight has to be perfect! Absolutely perfect!

Cheryl Dada walked to the pebble and kicked it harder. The pebble struck the security post window with a force that startled the sleepy guard.

"Hello!" The man stuck his head out of the stained window.

"Hello, Cheok," said Cheryl. "Sorry about that."

"It's okay lah. Where you going? The weather so hot today," said Cheok, holding a red battery-operated fan to his face.

"I'm going to get some flowers."

"Flowers?"

"Yes," said Cheryl, perturbed by the white blades that came very close to the security guard's unshaven face.

"For what?"

"They are for the party tonight," she said.

"Oh yah!" Cheok exclaimed. "Tonight big event… I think ang pows will also be very big this year. They cannot lose to last year. You think?"

Cheryl Dada smiled sagely.

"Must be lah. I think at least fifty," Cheok went on. "Cannot be lesser than last year mah."

"Fifty is good," said Cheryl.

"Eh what kind of party flower you getting anyway?" asked the security guard.

"Lilies, maybe."

Slouching back in his chair, he burst out: "Eh don't get gek huay hor. That one for dead people!"

Cheryl kept quiet, slightly smiling when he dropped the fan in a fit of laughter.

"Also better don't get jasmine. That one for praying!" Cheok guffawed, bobbing his head. "Fake flower also cannot hor!"

"Yes," said Cheryl with finality. He looked like one of those Japanese fortune cats: bulging eyes and jovial and fat.

Cheok was still laughing, verily proud of his joke. Cheryl was unmoved by the bit of humour. She found him uncouth and vulgar. Perhaps it was because he never tucked his shirt in. And he did not wear socks. It was also the way he mispronounced words, like the time he kept saying "penis" when he meant "finish", and how he said "supplies" instead of "surprise". He also snorted when he laughed. What an old Ah Beng, she thought.

"Have you seen Daniel?" asked Cheryl in an abrupt tone.

"What?" Cheok reached down to pick up the fan.

"Daniel. Have you seen him?"

"Cheh. I still thought what are you saying... Daniel is with the Myanmar woman lah," said Cheok, scratching his ear. "The nurse manager lor, who else."

"Yu Yu?"

"Yah, Yu Yu," he laughed. "I think they go Ang Mo Kio Hub buy drinks for tonight lah. They very gum you know—"

Cheryl said she supposed so.

"Aiya, I tell you that Yu Yu is—" Cheok paused, searching for the right word. "She is...how to say..." he tried again, putting the fan down.

She nodded detachedly, letting him go on.

How to say? Cheok thought harder, turning in his chair, looking left and right, as if the word were somewhere in the room. He was clicking his tongue. Tsk! What's the word!

"You know what is gum or not?"

Cheryl declined to entertain him.

"Aiyo you don't know ah? Gum...means like..."

She resented his tone. She could make out the thoughts forming in his mind and wished he did not find the words for them.

"You know what is lao niu chi nen cao?" asked Cheok hopefully.

Cheryl Dada shook her head.

Cheok glanced at her, wondering if she were Chinese. A Chinese who cannot speak Chinese? Funny leh, he thought. Dada's a funny surname too. Even if she married an Indian, she shouldn't forget her Chinese. What did she see in him? A big man who dresses like a geena, Cheok thought, recalling that her husband always wore a colourful checked shirt when he visited. He could not understand Mrs Dada's taste in men. It was just as well that she could not understand him too. Cheok guessed that their difference might be attributed to the fact that she was from an English school. One of those fake ang mohs.

Cheok was getting restless, rubbing the tip of his long pinkie nail. How to say? How to get her to understand?

Then, surrendering to the unbendable distance between them, for he thought in a different language from the one she spoke, he said, "Never mind lah. I also don't know how to say. Later Daniel come back I will tell him to find you."

He leaned back in his chair and picked up the fan again; she took it to be a sign that it was time to leave.

Cheryl Dada was relieved that the conversation was over. She waved a hand to say bye and continued walking. Daniel and Yu Yu must have gone to NTUC to get drinks, she thought remotely, as she passed by the iron gate again. She was pleased that they did not forget about the drinks and they were coming to her party tonight.

Daniel is on top of his job, she thought, walking around the set tables in the car park, and touching their surfaces to check if they were wiped down properly. He has grown so much, she thought again smilingly, pleased about his advancement and that there was not a speck of dust on the tables.

For the longest time Cheryl was worried for him. His degree in Social Work did not teach him how to manage people who were much older than he. He'll be out of here in a month, she remembered thinking at that time. He was 23 when he first arrived; his cheeks were still pink and glowing. How's this boy going to run the place? Cheryl had thought when she saw him stepping out of the taxi in his oversized suit and sneakers, and walking up to her and smiling genially. She was positive that HR made a mistake.

But then he stood in front of her, bowed slightly and extended his hand, saying in a strong, masculine voice: "Hello, I'm Daniel Chang. It's lovely to meet you."

Cheryl was taken aback; Lulu and the other women were as well. He had a commanding presence when he spoke. Though they did not understand most of what he was saying, the women found him very suave and gentlemanly. Fair-skinned and tall, endowed with slit eyes and pinkish lips, Daniel was a pretty boy who seemed to have stepped out of a Korean drama. Judy Chua went on to comment that he looked like Lee-something-something. Most residents and staff agreed. Although Cheryl Dada did not catch the reference, she, too, was of the opinion that he was good-looking. She tried but could not place his accent. It was not British; he sounded nothing like John Pitts. His voice was a rich baritone that was warm and mellow. It was intense and affirming, speaking to the heart more than the ears. It made up for the years that he had lacked in appearance, masking well the uncertainties of a fresh graduate.

No wonder he's a social worker, said Cheryl. She ambled through the last few tables and reached the raised platform that was going to be the stage for tonight's party. It made sense; the boy had a gift. Not everyone can reach the soul, she thought, especially when the soul was hardened like hers. Why, with that voice of his, he should be tonight's emcee. With a suit and tie, and some mousse on his hair, of course.

Mrs Dada was happy that Daniel had earned the respect of the residents and staff, of Yu Yu especially. The nurse manager was intimidating, very experienced in her field. She was hailed as the bona fide pioneer generation worker cum long service award winner in the home; the only one out of 156 staff who was on an E Pass. The rest of the nurses saw her as a model example and envied her PPR status, i.e. POTENTIAL PR. All these years working in the home had earned her not only a covetable status but also a lot, a lot of money. So much money—"She is a millionaire if she go home. And ah, she got no children also," said Lulu—that she could buy a taxi company and some land in Myanmar, and retire.

Yu Yu had been working in the home for 16 years and recently renewed her contract for another two. She had built a life here with friends as family, found her favourite places to hang out and food to eat. The nurse manager always said to the residents, "Madam, time to makan"; and "Let's go makan!" to her friends. She knew that block 630 sold vegetarian kway chap; block 108 had the best butter abalone mushroom; Teck Ghee food centre had the thickest and chewiest mee chiang kueh (which Leow Mei Ling often pestered her to buy); and block 628 had recently made headlines for one sumo big prawn noodle—prawns that were mistaken for baby lobsters! Singapore was Yu Yu's home. In fact, it might be better than back home.

This question of home, Cheryl Dada mulled over, leaving the unfinished stage and turning left to the open walkway that led to the bottom of the slope. This feeling of belonging kept her mind occupied as she walked along.

Living in this home all these years, people coming and going... Was this place, after all, home?

She was used to the blue and white colours; the long corridors; the terracotta roof. The place wasn't like one of those gated homes with railings and ramps everywhere. With all that healthcare equipment and aids, even the healthy and kicking would think they needed help. This place was different; the home was open and green.

I am happy here, thought Cheryl Dada; I'm more happy than I've ever remembered being. "This feels right," she said, as she started up the slope, heading towards the therapy centre. It was the only thing in a long time that actually felt right. This being here, alone. She was sick of thinking—all that thinking, thinking. No more racing thoughts, no more overactive mind. A woman can only do so much thinking before her thoughts become treacly sentiments. Cheryl Dada was going to try to go with her heart now. To listen to the still small voice—was that what they called it? From now on she would answer only to her heart. Too long had she left it yearning, unrequited. If it kept beating, even when she refused it, then it must want something. What was it—life? Death? Love? Which one did the heart want? Cheryl had no answer. But she was going to try feeling now.

"Feeling, feeling, feeling," Cheryl Dada chanted, setting the pace for the rest of the climb. She had her eyes on the near horizon dividing the road and the building ahead. One was the colour of asphalt; the other was cloudy grey.

Both were some kind of grey. What happened to colours? Modern aesthetics bored her. She hated the monochrome: black, white, grey. Didn't they decide to do away with black-and-white and sepia and all the vintage tints when they invented colour televisions? Why was multicolour good for the television but tacky for buildings and clothes? This world needs to be more consistent, she thought, stopping to catch her breath. All the grey around Cheryl Dada did not make the climb any easier. Apart from the blue sky, everything was gloomy. "Oh God! I cannot keep up," she lamented, trudging up the slope.

The city used to fascinate her—the old city with its colours and cacophony: the red brick National Library; the Van Kleef Aquarium; Hock Hiap Leong, where her mother used to bring her for lunch almost every Sunday when she was in primary school after church service in the morning. Thank God St Andrew's is still there, she thought. It could very well be up for demolition, or "urban planning", as they call it these days. But then again, secular as the country is, it surely would not risk offending anybody's god. Religious riots are as possible as racial riots. Maybe more catastrophic, for the weapons of the gods are fires and floods. One must not underestimate the divine and its emmets; the power of religious organisations. Cheryl remembered reading an article a few months earlier about churches getting together to wear white in solidarity against the...what was the word Judy Chua used? She was shouting in the dining hall: "Aiya God don't like those—" What was it? Cheryl thought, and shut her eyes to remember better. But Judy Chua was no Christian. The shrill voice belonged to someone else. She who said something about a thrice-holy God who did not like ah kuas. Anyway, better not to touch the people of God and their holy grounds.

Her stomach growled as she thought about char kuay teow and ice Horlicks. That was her must-order on Sundays. Hock Hiap Leong was almost always packed and smelled of grease and smoke. When they did get a table, Cheryl would guard it with her arms spread over the sticky marble top while her mother made the orders. Her mother told the uncle, "Mai hum"; Cheryl would follow suit and shout, "Mai hiam!" The uncle had a white towel wrapped around his neck like it was a scarf. The ceiling fan was way too high up.

Cheryl Dada continued up the slope more slowly. Lunch was after church and after MPH. While most kids her age went to the community library, she went to the MPH in town. She still remembered the big doors—half wood, half glass—that she did not have the strength to push open. Her mother would go before her and then disappear into the magazine section. Left alone for a couple of hours, Cheryl would find a space on the second floor near the Enid Blyton bookshelf, hidden away from the store people, so she could eat her jelly without being chased away. There she read *Charlie and the Chocolate Factory* and *Charlie and the Great Glass Elevator*. Her favourite book was *James and The Giant Peach*; she looked up to Miss Spider but did not like Mr Centipede as much. Her reading interest expanded from *The Adventures of Rupert* to *The Famous Five*; her last book was *Bridge to Terabithia*. But she never got to the end. She never found out what happened to Jesse because they stopped going to MPH when Times Bookshop first opened in Specialists' Centre; it stocked a more international magazine collection but no *Bridge to Terabithia*. Her mother refused to buy the book for her; she did not believe in buying books unless they were textbooks. But it was just as well, since Cheryl could not imagine the story without Leslie, Jesse without her.

These buildings... The buildings nowadays are awful, Cheryl Dada thought, stepping onto the walkway of the therapy centre. Looking at the gloomy walls in front of her, at the fake potted flowers (maybe Juwel could come over and plant some daisies or hibiscuses here), she sighed in despair, thinking instead of the old police station on Hill Street. That was Singapore—diverse and vibrant. Back in the day to be colourful was to be multi-racial: Malay; Indian; Chinese; and Eurasian. We're beige and brown and yellow and white. These days the buzzword is cosmopolitanism. So many shades of yellow and brown; so many degrees of fairness. Different kinds of Chinese people, different kinds of Malays, different kinds of Indians. Also different types of Asians: maids; foreign workers; construction workers; "tiongs"; Malaysians. White people are easier to categorise; they are simply Expats, even if they cannot speak proper English. A Lithuanian gets as big a smile as an American in the stores.

Diversity was getting too complicated for Cheryl Dada. She did not know what race she was any more. She was Chinese, also one quarter Peranakan; but as a Dada, was she still Chinese? Was she considered a cosmopolitan person? All the colours and categories left her confused.

Colourful means something else these days, she contemplated, as she reached the entrance. The grey building with the gaudy signboard that said *ELDERFLOWER THERAPY CENTRE* was an eyesore.

Cheryl Dada had in mind the Peranakan shophouses. They were very colourful. She adored the animal reliefs and floral motifs, the ceramic tiles and wooden window shutters. For a very short while she had lived in a similar terraced house, one with timber window frames and peony tiles. Cheryl remembered a couple of things: the super-hard chairs that hurt her backside, the spacious and well-aired hall. That was when her great-grandmother was still around. The house looked nothing like that blue house on Neil Road she saw on the heritage excursion. Maybe Lao Ma's house wasn't Peranakan enough, she thought; maybe they were not rich enough. And what about herself? Was she Peranakan enough? Cheryl Dada pondered, pausing at the entrance of the building; the air conditioner vent was blowing cold air on her.

Peranakan meant little these days. Not much to Cheryl Dada anyway. She could not speak Malay and she hated buah keluak. She also did not like Nonya dumplings, preferring the sweet kee zhang. Being Peranakan did not affect her. But actually nothing was affective enough, nothing was important enough to pique her interest. She had been feeling especially dull lately, listless, no drive—or hope. Cheryl Dada seemed to lack the lust for life. For too long she had been schooled in the field of moderation that the lust for anything did not come easy to her. She attributed this purity trait to church and being in a single-sex school. Of course her mother and all that flower talk about women being jasmines and baby's breaths—in short, little white flowers—played a big part too. Perhaps this was also a blessing in disguise. For if she seldom felt lust, she also was seldom ashamed. Therein was the strength of the little white flower: she was unfazed, standing erect and bright, carefree and comfortable in the shadows. Her mother might not have foreseen the brazenness that Cheryl had adopted in her adulthood, and most certainly would have regretted her moral teachings had she known that her daughter did not shy away from the covert. For Cheryl was, for example, unashamed of sex in her later years. She did not understand the taboo, the appeal, nor the shame associated with it. Assuredly, she was no libertine; there were no men or sane women around even if she had impulses. Cheryl Dada would have been a hippie outside the home. But here she was ungratified, with little hope for action.

Walking into the therapy centre, Cheryl thought about the difference between hope, expectation and wishful thought. Which of them has feathers? What paralyses but still beats death? God forbid there be no difference.

Hope, she heard someone say, is a confident expectation of the future. Her mother, in old age, used to quote Isaiah: "Those who hope in the Lord will renew their strength." Like how the hope of finding some lilies gave Cheryl the strength to climb up the treacherous slope to the therapy centre. Her mother had a different idea of hope. She told her that a baby could be the hope for a marriage going downhill. That Cheryl was the saving grace of her parents' relationship. Her mother said she was going to leave Cheryl's father but had abandoned the thought when she found out she was pregnant again. Things got better after that; husband and wife were talking more. They even took a family photo that still hung in her mother's room. She said it was like falling in love once more, the honeymoon phase repeated.

Cheryl was too young to remember what it had been like when her father died. She did not remember seeing her mother weep. She probably did not even see much of her since her grandmother was her main caregiver. All they had left of her father was the black leather sofa he was wont to sleep on. It was sunken in from the weight of his body and took the vague shape of his pudgy frame. It reeked of tobacco. Her mother got rid of the sofa when they moved out.

Block 316 was stuck with the en bloc redevelopment notice in 1995. That was hope for her mother, financially at least. Cheryl, too, was relieved, for she was also servicing the housing loan. It was all very timely. Her mother had been retrenched the year before and taking more allowance from Cheryl. She needed money and the government showed up: the compensation was more than the subsidised cost of the new flat. Her mother was happy that she got to keep the rest of the sales money for her retirement but was upset that the house was small. She also complained that living on the 25th floor was hazardous (What if a fire broke out? Was she supposed to climb all the way down on her own?) and that the lift made her ears uncomfortable. Cheryl hardly stayed over so she did not mind the height or downgrade. She only wished they had kept the sofa.

Cheryl Dada had turned into a long corridor that connected the lobby to the courtyard. She walked hurriedly but carefully, sticking close to the wall to give way to the oncoming traffic.

"Gosh, careful," she cried, shunning a woman in her wheelchair who yelled back, "You then careful lah!"

"This place is too tight!" she said, exasperatedly.

A nurse pushing a trolley of blood pressure monitors passed by and smiled in agreement.

"Hazardous!" said Cheryl Dada under her breath. They should expand this space the next time they renovate the whole area, she thought, trying to count the number of renovations in the past year.

"Careful!" Cheryl Dada backed up against the wall of the corridor to make way for a speeding stretcher. "Look where you're going," she said to the men in masks, her words accompanied by the creaking sound of unoiled wheels.

"Careful, careful!" Cheryl cried out to another nurse passing her by, nearly knocking over her tray of tubes and bottles.

"Aiyo, careful lah, Madam!"

Excuse me—Cheryl wanted to shout out, but was distracted by the wheelchair that was swerving in her direction. Its wheel rammed against one of her toes.

"Fuck! For God's sake!" she shrieked, instantly withdrawing her foot and kicking the silver rim. "Ouch!" she cried, bending down to check her toe. "What the hell is wrong with you?"

The cursing continued, but her voice was drowned by the tumult of voices, of shoes stamping on the ground and wheels squeaking.

"What the hell!" she yelled, pulling herself up and for the first time looking away from her throbbing toe to meet the adversary, eye to eye.

"What is wrong—"

Cheryl Dada stood still for a couple of seconds until the sight fully registered in her mind: the slightly trembling hands, the drooping head, the runny nose. The lips were twitching; the woman wanted to say something:

"Sh...shh...shorr—"

"No, no," Cheryl interjected.

"Shorr...orr...eee..."

"No, *I'm* sorry," Cheryl reached down and said into her ear.

She knew right away. Most telling was the blank stare. The same emotionless stare had convinced her that her mother was gone years before her body finally caught up and shut down. The woman's eyes reflected a similar vacant look of hope frozen. Not the new beginning, clean slate type of blankness. These were fish eyes; dead eyes.

Must be someone from block D, thought Cheryl Dada impulsively, seized by the fear that one day it could be her turn. "Ten per cent of the forty thousand people suffering from dementia in this country are below the age of sixty." She had memorised this fact from a newspaper article and copied it on her wall to ward off complacency. While the odds were not really against her, and she did not yet display substantial symptoms, Cheryl's trepidation was justified, for there was indeed a history of early deaths in her family. Her great-grandmothers had passed away in their late fifties; her grandmother too. Her mother had lived longer and made it to her sixties, but Cheryl had regarded her dead when she received the doctor's final report. It was easier that way.

"D for Dementia," the women would joke in the dining hall. They laughed heartily because laughter was not a sign of degeneration. They pettifogged and rolled about in their wheelchairs, reluctantly went for OT and PT because a quick mind and fine motor skills were not signs either. Whatever the women's ages, there were bound to be some memory lapses. Some residents pretended to remember while others made up the past. Cheryl too, though she thought herself to be more selective in remembering than forgetful. The point was nobody wanted to be moved to block D. But this woman in the wheelchair—she probably did not have a choice. The signs were too obvious.

Cheryl could not help but profile the woman, as if evincing her condition would relight her blank, distant eyes.

She dug from her memory the scraps of medical facts and snippets of what she had seen in her years in the home. The woman could be suffering from vascular or frontotemporal dementia; she could be plagued by a mixed type. It was hard to say, for dementia is merely a general term for brain-draining disorders like Alzheimer's, Lewy Body Disease and Parkinson's. Cheryl knew none of that information would mitigate the symptoms of the woman's affliction, delay the inevitable and already lingering end, but Cheryl Dada trusted in individual experience and the woman's life had to be told.

Cheryl thought to herself: now she's experiencing muscle rigidity—that means no more writing. Her head's inclining to the left, unblinkingly choosing sides, as though the world on the right were dismal. Whichever side it was, Cheryl hoped that it was the one facing the window so there would be more sunshine in her life. Back in her room, the woman would not be able to wash herself so the room would stink. But it wasn't just dirt and sweat; the room would stink of poop. She would have to endure long periods of constipation and disturbed bowel movements. At least two nurses would change her panties a few times a day, and in due time when the incontinence finally got out of hand they'd give her diapers, maybe hook her up to a urine bag. But one bag would not be enough. Soon she would have difficulty breathing; her mucous would be too thick and get stuck inside her lungs. Another drainage bag for that. In the advanced stage, she would not recognise that there was food in her mouth and thus be unable to decide to swallow.

A feeding tube would be inserted into her stomach. She might cough up the blenderised food or saliva. The healthcare staff would tie a towel around her neck to manage the mess. It would be the full works: diapers and bibs. The victim of dementia would live long enough to be like a baby again, for it could take years from the onset of the disease to the belated end. First, rigid muscles; then, rigor mortis. And reincarnation, unless she was a believer in heaven and the streets of gold.

Cheryl searched the woman's neck for some sign of divinity and faith. A pendant, a crucifix or talisman, or perhaps a yellow string tied around her wrist. One must have some belief in a higher order in such situations. It is the only viable support system. Both Mrs Rohan and Poh Choo had converted to Catholicism for this reason. Because once the affliction is full blown, the afflicted is unreachable. And if anything could reach out in absolute and abject solitude, it must be God.

Unfortunately there was no necklace or bracelet. Perhaps she had something sewn in her gown or fastened to her chair. Cheryl would have continued with her search but a nurse intercepted; her hands gripped the wheelchair handles tightly, whisking the woman away from her.

Feeling guilty, Cheryl wanted to shout out an apology to her, but the words that came out strung a prayer from memory: "Lord, touch this life which You have made, now and forever." She was about to follow up with a prayer to assuage her guilt but was yet again interrupted by a familiar face.

"Good afternoon, Cheryl!" shouted the man in a white suit.

"Hi, John," Cheryl Dada shouted back. And regretted it immediately.

The rotund man with a full head of blonde hair was waving to her. She was not used to seeing him outside, in public or in the crowd. They usually met in his office, a cream-painted room with a long black sofa and green armchair. There was also a desk that he never used.

The man walked clumsily towards her. His face grew bigger as he came closer. Without his spectacles, his eyes looked larger and more blue.

"How are you?" he said, leaning down to speak to her. His breath smelled of onions.

Cheryl stood very upright, and held in her breath.

"I'm going to get some flowers," she said, looking to the wall behind him, averting the blue eyes.

"Grand! What are you getting—roses or sunflowers?" The cheery voice was detached from the expressionless face.

She said hesitantly: "I was thinking...maybe lilies."

"How interesting!"

He was doing it again, she thought, picking apart her words rather than listening.

"I don't think there are lilies," John said with a wave of his hand. "But that's an interesting choice. We'll discuss that next time."

No more next time, Cheryl was inclined to say. She did not want to see him; she did not want to go into that room. She hated how he watched her body slump or lean back, how he commented on her every word and gesture. His thin silver glasses rested so low on his nose that when he looked at her, his blue eyes were divided—half normal and half enlarged. He would say to her, "How are you?" when she entered his lair. "How's your week?" "How's the day going?" The worst of his greetings was "You're all right?" Cheryl never knew what the appropriate answer to that was. "Good," or "Okay," she would say awkwardly, her reply based on the weather. Regardless of what she said, John would always have a follow-up question ready in his mind—a motivation speech, a sheet of paper for her in his green folder. He also had something to say when she was quiet or restless in the sofa that was sometimes still warm from the previous person. Sometimes she could smell the person even after she was gone. Like how she knew Cheng Hong from block B had been there because she could sniff out the jasmine tea scent. When she tried to confirm this information with John, he turned it around and asked her why she felt the need to know. The conversation after that became about control and the need to let go of things. All she wanted to know was if Cheng Hong had been there. But John had to go on for another hour before allowing her to go home. This must be what it meant to make a mountain out of a molehill. Even if she did not show up, John would still be able to write a report and make something up. That was his expertise.

"Well—" The voice broke the silence. "You'd better get going then," John said brightly. "See you later!"

What did he mean by later? Did he know about the party? Remember my party, Cheryl wanted to say; the more the merrier, she tried to convince herself.

Cheryl let out a big smile, relieved at his departure. Why do ang mohs talk so much? she thought, watching him return to the crowd, his sandy-haired head above the rest, bobbing along. He did not have to walk over to her; she wished he hadn't. She needed her space. What else did he want? His words resounded in her mind: "We'll discuss that next time." No, she should have rebutted. There was not going to be a next time this week. They had already met once. Ang mohs just don't get it, she thought, pressing against the group of nurses that were coming towards her. (One had said, "Hi, Mrs Dada!" "Hey," Cheryl responded quickly, albeit distractedly.) All those busybody questions... What was the point of getting to the problem when there was no getting out of it? Might as well keep quiet. What was the use of talking? Talk is cheap—did he not know this? Silence is golden—did he not learn that in med school? Maybe they didn't teach that in England, she thought. "How are you?" he would ask before the session. "How are you?" he would ask midsession. "How are you?" he would ask at the end of the session. Not well, obviously. Why did he think she was there? For fun?

John talks too much, she mumbled, walking on. He was always rattling on about England, about behaviour, about feelings. Why did a big man like him keep talking about such stuff? Why did he keep wanting to talk about life? Was life not evident enough? It was for her.

For what it was worth, John told good stories. If only he would stop throwing out big words that she did not understand. There was something about effect—or was it affect? CBT or DBT or PPT—Cheryl liked how they rhymed so nicely. There was also SRT. CBT was her favourite: it was code for drawing. But the real highlight of the sessions was John's educational stories. He was the English version of the Professor Tortoise who knew everything. Occasionally, on some Fridays, he would wear the pair of dark round-framed glasses that made him look even more like the tortoise. Professor Tortoise was Clare's favourite cartoon character, second to Dexter. Clare always liked the smart ones. But no, Cheryl must not tell John that.

John had a lot of stories about England. Sometimes she wondered why he was here when he was such a patriot. He told her that Scotch is exclusively from Scotland and whisky is spelled without the "e". He also said the north of England has a lot of white people and they speak a dialect called Geordie. She asked if it's a dialect like Teochew but he said no. Geordie is English with a funny accent. "The vowels are flatter," he said. Instead of mum, it's mam in the north. And it's not up, it's ooup. OOOOUP. High ooup in the sky.

John was not like them—the northerners. He did not speak Geordie. "I speak the Queen's English," he once told her. Jonathan Thomas Pitts was born in a place called Cornwall, which was the southernmost part of the country. He said he went to Eton, then to Oxford. "Like Cameron," he said with pride. But the only other British celebrity that Cheryl Dada knew was Mr Bean.

From him Cheryl learned that the Republic of Ireland is not part of the United Kingdom but Northern Ireland is. Also part of the United Kingdom is Scotland, the northernmost part of the country, although it has its own flag and currency. John said that Scotland has the best water and brews the best tea; that water in the midlands and South England is hard. Cheryl never knew water could be hard—surely he didn't mean like ice? He also told her that tea with milk is an English thing. Back home they call it white tea, not teh. The English use proper milk for their tea; not milk powder or condensed milk. He said no self-respecting English would drink tea strained from a sock; but if it only costs a dollar, why not? When she asked him about teh-o, John said the correct term is black tea. But the woman at Toast Box gave her a look of disdain when she had asked for black tea, so she stuck with teh-o. Sometimes she would order teh-o-kosong, but she refused to drink teh.

Tea with milk, she thought sardonically. So particular for what? For really, English or Chinese, white or black or yellow, a cup of tea or teh, then and now, with or without milk; John sitting in his armchair, she at the edge of the sofa, the table between them—was that not the nature of harmony? People existed together precisely because of differences. Same, but all different, she thought. Same brains; different minds. But difference is difficult to talk about, so we harp on being the same. We are one people, one nation, one Singapore.

Harmony, Cheryl Dada reflected on the word. Huh… mourn…nay, she thought, walking to the end of the corridor. Racial huh mourn nay. Or yay. If such harmony existed, it was an enforced one. Racial Harmony Day, for one, was perfunctory and preventive rather than celebratory. In the name of harmony, many things were forced. She thought reminiscently about having worn a kebaya to some gala; it had been a tough decision, a toss-up between the Peranakan garb and a cheongsam. Both were just dresses, neither particularly significant to her. But since her grandmother had worn a kebaya once or twice, and given that the SIA uniform was tried and tested, Cheryl went with it: a jade and gold batik sarong; a mint blouse that was much lighter than it looked, probably due to the translucency of the material, was ornamented with a butterfly brooch with emerald eyes and wings. The whole thing wrapped her tight; she could barely walk properly, taking small steps in those heels— Was she wearing heels?

The thought jolted her. Heels with the kebaya? They must have been in an irresistible shade of green, otherwise she would not have gone against the tradition. It was more like her to wear Mama's hand-stitched sequin flats.

In retrospect, Cheryl regretted some of the green. Green used to make her feel closer to her Peranakan roots. She thought it was the cultural colour—the colour of pandan, Nonya kaya, petai, lemongrass. When she was younger, she'd make it a point to wear something green whenever possible, that she might be reminded of her roots.

Nothing harmonious about the kebaya, Cheryl began again, arriving at the end of the corridor. What did it mean—this display of people wearing their differences on their skin? What about people of the same colour outside but different insides? Harmony swept real differences under the rug. Harmony is bad for those who are different from people like John, she thought as she stepped out of the therapy centre. All difference behind her: nurses in blue and green; elder women in gowns; sleepy faces; droopy faces; grouchy faces; faces damp with sweat; faces with tubes taped to their skin; her own face pale and wrinkled. She, Cheryl Dada, who used to be distinguished, was now like them, another face in the crowd, a mere statistic. She was one of those old folks living harmoniously under one roof.

V

The corridor opened into a veranda. Cheryl Dada felt as if the place were larger than its form, as if each pillar extended beyond the wooden roof, as if all the stone tables were semi-excavated fossils from another time; the world, she felt, had become boundless and the air was let in. Finally, the afternoon breeze was gathering, eddying round the four corners of the veranda.

Near the edge of the veranda was a lime plant that Cheryl often picked from. Since her mission today was to get flowers, she would only look, take inventory of the ripe limes and leave them for tomorrow. The outdoor ceiling fan blew directly on the waxy leaves; and they trembled, as though the rays of the sun were dancing on them.

No limes today, Cheryl Dada reminded herself, hands in her pockets, as she walked along the pebbles that lined the edge of the wooden floor. Her head brushed against the drooping leaves of the purple and white orchids that were hanging from the wooden beam above. They looked wrinkly and sad, high up and far away from the periwinkles and ixoras. Cheryl had heard from Juwel that Vanda Miss Joaquim was tough to grow, more difficult to care for than the normal orchids. Something about it being a hybrid flower and requiring heavy fertilising.

Why bother? she thought, leaning against the corner post. Now that they were leathery and limp, was it worth the trouble and effort? Nah, they're not worth it, thought Cheryl Dada, straightening her ailing back. Not the wilted, old ones. Why bother with the dying flowers?

Cheryl Dada preferred cactuses. She had bought a round, thorny one from IKEA on her last home leave. Cactuses are resilient, bloom on neglect, and are easy to maintain. Fuss free and evergreen, they're plants for the minimalist, for those who want some life in the house but ambivalent about exactly what kind of life. Cheryl Dada could vouch for the cactus; she had one sitting on her windowsill and it was indeed thriving in an unostentatious manner, without fertilisers or much water, without any of those froufrou stuff like colourful pebbles or gnomes. Andes—she had named it—was surviving as well as it would have in the desert. Andes was ugly: it had no leaves and was prickly, but it was going to last for a long time. And that was the most important thing—that it would last. Cheryl Dada liked Andes very much; she adored a simple life with little expectations and less strife.

Pursuit; empty pursuit, she thought, feeling a mild breeze on her face, and turning round as behind her an orchid pot fell to the floor. Another one bites the dust; the exposed roots, the scattered soil and ceramic shards, and pigeons wobbling on the veranda. Life and death, thought Cheryl Dada. What's lost? she said, ponderingly, gazing at the silhouettes of the trees; she thought about her mother's dream, of her first child, the primeval promise that her last could not fulfil. She must have been disappointed, thought Cheryl Dada; her whole life had circled around her child like a vulture, nudging her to pick up the leftovers of her unfinished dream, and she had said, "Why can't you be more sensible? Why can't you think about me?" But look where all that thinking had got her? Nowhere. Cheryl walked over to the pot of purple orchids hanging from another beam. Hope, she thought, rests in death.

Betterment is a myth, she now realised, tingling all over, replaying in her mind the scene in her bedroom: the night she chose Accountancy over Literature—how her mother had weighed up the pros and cons for her and handed her the application form, and she thought about how her life could have easily turned the other way—no calculating, no marrying. Cheryl Dada reached for the smallest flower in the hanging pot and, pulling it towards her, broke the bud from its stem; "If only!" she said, but it fell to the ground.

If only Cheryl Dada could have it all over again. She would have been strong, as a kid strong enough to do PE and jump ropes. She would have enjoyed zero point and hopscotch. She might have been, if she could start over, more athletic like Sarah, with her angular built and slender legs. (How she ran! How free she was!) She would have been, if she were 13 again, more opinionated—interested in debating and Speech and Drama; fought with the neighbour's boys who laughed at her pigtails and shot frogs at them with her catapult. She would have run, yes she would have run with Sarah across the field in the rain—shirtless and barefoot—screaming at the top of her lungs. She would have jumped into drains and bushes to forage for saga seeds and keep them in tiny glass jars for Valentine's Day. Like Sarah, she would have been brave. She would have insisted that she had done nothing wrong, that the form teacher was crazy, that they were just kids playing in the toilet cubicle. But she was never that kid whom Sarah was. They'd never be those kids again.

Looking at her hands that were blotched with sunspots, Cheryl Dada had the strangest sense of being unified, of two warring natures conjoined without confusion. Blue veins crawled over the skin that had lost its sheen. The backs of her hands were like badly-stencilled porcelain ware waiting to be broken, as though longing to return to its potter's hands. Yet when she held her palms up, the skin was soft and supple as clay. The heart line, still trident, was engraved when she was 13.

"Ah Le next time zor tai tai." The words of her grandmother attached themselves to the lines on her hand.

Cheryl remembered: the knobbly fingers, the tickling sensation, the Teochew-ridden English. Mama must have been about this age when she began falling ill. Cheryl could still see her slumped in the rocking chair, her hand motioning her to come closer. Mama had this smile and warmth that was seldom seen in the old ladies around here. She would say, "Ah Le, come here. Come sit beside Mama," then grab Cheryl by the nearer hand and examine her palm.

Mama's hands were gigantic and puffy. Her rings, like binds, were holding the fingers in check, lest they exploded.

She was about to cry, she felt. Instinctively, Cheryl reached for the pendant that was tucked inside her shirt and traced its edges. Mama had given her her emerald ring but it was too large to fit any of her tiny fingers—so Cheryl had worn it as a pendant since. Mama sold the gold rings and her favourite purple jade ring, but she kept the wedding band. As her health began to deteriorate, the family's wealth shrinking accordingly, even the last ring—her only memento of Ah Gong, aside from a couple of black-and-white photographs—seemed to be slipping away. It was only with the help of a piece of tape wedged between the ring and her shrivelling finger that the tarnished silver band did not come off. Without most of the rings, Mama's hands appeared naked.

"Ah Le next time zor tai tai." The words—her grandmother's foretelling—which she could not fully comprehend when she was a kid had come to pass. Rich as she was, with many people at her beck and call, Cheryl Dada still had to get the flowers. A tai tai in this Ang Mo Kio home did not entitle her to as many privileges. But she did have a private room—which was the mark of affluence.

Which flowers to get? she thought, stepping down on the grass. She hoped there would be lilies, especially the white ones. Sunflowers would do; red roses would be lovely too. But Cheryl Dada had a hunch that the only flowers left in the garden would be the azaleas. She might get some rosemary sprigs from the herb garden on the way back. They would spruce up the red and white tables.

It was her mother who had told her that a woman is like a flower: a pure and white and small flower. Her pep talk was flowery. She was very fussy about species and colours. Women, most women, are like little white flowers. Only a few are likened to the white rose and lily in the valley; and Cheryl was not that—not as beautiful, not as favoured as the girls in school and in the neighbourhood.

"Don't be stupid. You think you so good is it?" her mother would stress. Be humble, be like most girls. "You are strong and pretty in bunches," she complimented, though the remark sounded more motivational in nature and tone than praise. Cheryl was one of those little white flowers in a bouquet, a filler flower. One that was functional rather than ornamental, like the elderflower that's medicinal as well as nutritional, made into teas and syrups, treated like an herb and a garnish.

From her mother she learned that her petals would wither and flake off when she got older. So she had to stay white and pretty, stay in a bunch, until someone plucked her and brought her home. "Don't give yourself away," said her mother. But who was she going to give herself to? She was in a girls' school and all her friends were girls. And she was not allowed to go out after school. Weekends were spent at home too. Did she mean the neighbour boys? Or her twin cousins Han Yang and Han Yew? That would have been incestuous. What was she thinking? God, what was she thinking? How many petrifying and obscene scenarios did she have to conjure in her mind in order to psych herself into being so protective, so motherly? Cheryl shuddered at the thought of her thoughts.

A mother's mind runs very wild, Cheryl realised later in her life. It must have been, as they say, a mother's instinct, which turned out to be primal and imaginative. Once the child starts to blossom, her breasts pink and budding beneath her first bralet, the mother becomes watchful. Cheryl understood this; she too had become watchful because she knew what puberty did to young girls. She often found herself becoming the mother she hated. The more she tried to stop herself, the more she resembled her. So she gave up on motherhood; in doing so, she gave up the child that would have been her daughter, the Cheryl to her mother.

Walking in the yard, Cheryl Dada saw many mothers. Some were wheeled by younger women, presumably their daughters; some were struggling to walk, their wedding bands loose, knocking against the walking canes. Cheryl bent her head low and kept walking. The sight of mothers scared her. She could not bear even a wee reminder of the woman.

The path cut in the grass ran straight to the back garden, bringing Cheryl past the recreational ground where women were exercising and unwinding; some were sitting in their chairs, doing nothing. There was a band playing down the water fountain and the screeches drifted towards her.

One did not need to look up to know that it was the erhu group: Soh Lay Hoon, Leung Wing Man, Yong Ching Yee, the sisters Gina and Gracie Koh. They usually gathered at this time of the day, thrice a week, same place and same tunes, always the few Huang Fei Hong theme songs. Routines were important for the senior women: the structured activities provided a sense of control for they who had little agency in so many areas of their lives. The Koh sisters, as a case in point, chose to join the group over the ukulele ensemble because they thought that they could easily master the erhu due to their familiarity with the violin. Switching from classical to kung fu film music was difficult but at least they could use their bowing techniques and feel relevant. Gina and Gracie were determined to become erhu virtuosos even though they loathed Chinese orchestral music. Such commitment and, to a lesser extent, contentment seemed to be achieved best in the scarcity of options.

Cheryl walked along, thinking about the changes the sisters had to make in order to learn and play those horrendous tunes. Soh Lay Hoon could have added other songs to the repertoire but she was too big a fan of kung fu dramas. That Jet Li's a Singaporean was something she harped on all the time—which was also her excuse to celebrate local heroes, as Daniel had explained to Gina and Gracie Koh when they aired their unhappiness regarding Soh Lay Hoon's song choices. This information somehow reached the ears of Mrs Rohan, who passed it on to Felicia Phua and Chin Siew Eng; by the time it reached Cheryl and the rest of the women, they were told that Soh Lay Hoon and her followers were communists and Daniel was a spy working for them, that the wordless Chinese songs were relaying propaganda.

Soh Lay Hoon was the home wrecker. Thankfully she was a day care client and so Cheryl had little contact time with her. Her dislike for Soh Lay Hoon had to do with her deep-seated resentment towards the day care people who came in and out of the home as they wished and assumed they had as much right as she who was here for good. They were just passing through; they had no business whatsoever in the home's affairs.

Their only direct encounter, which was enough to make a lasting impression on Cheryl, was about this time last year when Soh Lay Hoon wanted to put up a performance for National Day, suggesting that the group play "Home" and the national anthem on the erhu. Cheryl objected immediately, but Soh Lay Hoon stood her ground, which resulted in a heated argument; the two women argued in different languages and did not appear to share the same musical preference. In the end, the non-resident was victorious; Cheryl gave in on condition that there would be no such travesty next year. Today Soh Lay Hoon would keep her side of the bargain and leave after practice.

Cheryl Dada reached the allotment within a few minutes. The humble garden gate had no bolt, no lock, only a sign nailed to it that said TRESPASSERS WILL BE COMPOSTED. As if that would keep the wild boars out.

Cheryl Dada was no trespasser; she was the donor, one of its rightful owners. She took a few steps and gently pushed the gate. Its hinges were squeaking and the paint on the wood was chipping.

"Juwel needs to fix this," she said, dragging her finger over the jagged edges of the gate. This is too flimsy, she thought, and the wood is splintered. It's not going to keep anything out of the garden. Cheryl Dada lifted her eyes to the overgrown land behind the fence and wondered what was hiding in those bushes. What's hiding in the...*PROTECTED AREA?* Cheryl Dada focused on the red signboard. The bold white text glared at her. Was this new? She did not remember seeing it yesterday. *NO ADMITTANCE TO UNAUTHORISED PERSONS.* The white-painted figure of a man—was it a policeman or an army guard?—was mildly intimidating. It was his rifle that demanded obedience.

What could be so precious in the tangle of ungrazed land that required tight security? Cheryl Dada wondered; and went over the kinds of dangers in the area: there was talk of wild boars, snakes, and recently there were reports of a bunch of otters in Bishan Park. There had been the dead body in the water tank but that was old news. She heard about the breakout of tuberculosis in Avenue 4, although such danger could not be warded off by sturdy fences or men with guns. What were they trying to keep out? To the right of the field was a canal—were they afraid of illegal immigrants climbing out from secretly-dug tunnels? Was that even plausible? It was plausible, she thought.

On the far left was a primary school; Cheryl Dada was sure that students posed no threats. Maybe they were trying to deter unruly teenagers from the HDB area from playing football in the field. Worse—it suddenly occurred to Cheryl Dada—the man in white was pointing the rifle at her. It was trying to keep her out, keep them out; a warning to those who wanted to leave. For the only way out of here, out of the blue and white house, if not via the van or ambulance or—touch wood!—a hearse, was to climb the fence and cross over the field to the other side to civilisation. It must have been the two that got away last year. The sign was preventive, no doubt enforced with hidden cameras.

The red and white warning was an eyesore, rude and uncalled for. Did the man with a rifle honestly think he could stop anyone of them from leaving if they really wanted to? About that he was wrong. This was not Woodbridge; they were not locked up in that way. There were no great walls to scale, no barbed wires—the residents were allowed the bit of dignity that reminded them of their humanity. For to the residents—and Cheryl was thinking about herself—leaving was only a matter of time; and it was going to be a spectacular and transcendental departure. So, why would she escape? Cheryl was sure that the ones who got away, the ones whom Management did not want to name, were staff. The women would have known if it was a neighbour; they always knew when one of them disappeared overnight and what it meant when her long lost next-of-kin suddenly showed up the next day. Those two that went away...they were not one of them.

Why point the rifle at the helpless? Cheryl Dada thought. She was half-resigned, turning her eyes from the red and white board to the surrounding green expanse, which seemed to stand for the unbridgeable distance between the man with the rifle and herself. Why single out those who were already left behind? There was no way she could be like them living in those letter-box units, no way she could defend herself against the rifle or hold up one of her own. No way to hit the reset button.

Finding her habitual resignation give way to a welling righteousness, her body unexpectedly overcome by rage, Cheryl Dada made her way to the fence and locked her fingers into the green wired netting. She took a long, deep breath and shook the fence with every erg of energy she could summon.

"Fuck you! All of you fucking people!"

She tugged and tugged at the fence, attacking the void and screaming into nothingness. "Bloody hell. Damn this place!"

As soon as the last words left her mouth, fatigue came upon her and she released her grip on the netting. Slowly, step by step, she moved away from the fence and caught her breath. Then Cheryl Dada tucked her hands into her pockets and resumed her journey, walking towards the greenhouse. She kept her eyes on the path, taking care not to step on any snails in her way.

On the way there she wondered what they were going to do with the protected land. It had been there for the longest time, at least for the past seven years, and was still undeveloped. It's unlike the land authorities to leave such vast space alone for so long, she thought, tramping about the vegetation, the greenhouse in sight.

They are going to build a hotel, she surmised. Heartland tourism could be the next big thing. Just look at Ang Mo Kio Hub. Most of the healthcare staff hung out there in their free time.

It was a decent greenhouse, small but not too shabby. As she approached, it dawned on her that Juwel had built the entire thing from scratch with plywood and PVC pipes. Looking around, she was amazed by his contribution to the home. Before Juwel came, the garden had been a wretched-looking green space behind the kitchen where the staff would go for smoke breaks. Lucky's kennel was also there. If not for Juwel's greenhouse, Management would have put Lucky down to save the trampled garden.

For all that work we're not paying him enough, Cheryl Dada thought. Juwel, Vikash, Lulu and the whole lot of them—they were paid peanuts. But who was she to judge when she would have called them out and demanded that their salaries be docked if they did any less? Besides it was she who added to their workload, more so than the average resident did. So much work, so much effort. Why did they care? Did they really care, or was it about the money? Perhaps they truly took pride in their work. If this was home to them, then it made sense that they would strive to make it a better place. Because of them the country has smoother roads, brighter lights, trees that remain at a certain height, trees that never seem to shed. Still, in spite of her willingness to befriend them, Cheryl Dada kept a distance from the foreign workers. She thought that they always stared a little too long, their lips too eager to smile—as if they wanted something from her. But she could not say exactly why she felt this way.

Friendliness was suspect; indifference was the norm. It was true that Cheryl Dada preferred neutrality to kindness; she thought that being rude and snappy was sometimes considered more genuine than being friendly. Most acts of kindness towards her were often misinterpreted, for she could not understand that which was unfamiliar to her.

Only a few weeks ago she had lashed out at a schoolboy who had given up his seat on the train to her. The poor kid was almost in tears, but Cheryl Dada felt certain that she was the wronged one. For she did not need any priority, she did not need pity.

"Stand up for what?" she interrogated, although she already knew that he stood up because he saw her as lacking in something. "Do I look weak?" Cheryl Dada went on. Her limp and slow gait did not give him the right to judge her old and sickly. "I'm not that old," she asseverated, and continued: "Do I look like an ah ma?" The boy remained silent, guilty, cowering in terror.

The boy exited as soon as the train arrived at the next station. Cheryl Dada exited at the following station and insisted that Lulu take her home. Her day was already ruined. No shopping or walking was going to improve her mood.

Mrs Dada was a cliché. She knew that she was reinforcing the stereotype, but she acted out just for the heck of it. There was no better time than now. She could be unreasonable. She could rage against the dying of the light. Rage, rage! Fight, defy, fight the dying flame. Rage was hers by right and fact. Seniority was often confused with superiority in this country; and old age was a privilege to be exercised, not preserved and bottled up in a crematorium. She could whine and stamp her feet as she pleased, she could say whatever she wanted. If the nation had a look, it was like hers: childish; spiteful; but nonetheless pacifistic. Frustration and angst had an expression and people wore it on their faces. Cheryl Dada blamed the heat and haze.

It was only natural, given the culture in which she was raised, to be suspicious of people. Everyone had a real face, her mother told her, and a face they hid from others. The equivalent of a wolf in sheep's disguise. But why do we judge others by their actions and ourselves by our intentions? Perhaps her mother was right all along: "Faith it till you make it."

Standing in front of the greenhouse, Cheryl Dada was still in awe. With only a ladder and his bare hands, Juwel had managed to lug those glass panels up to form the semi-transparent roof. He even part-cladded the sides with weatherboards and draped plastic sheeting over the windows. The garden should have been named after him, instead of the Garden City Fund.

Coming up to the door, there was a furry brown board nailed to it. Cheryl Dada stopped to examine. It was like one of those bulletin boards in Clare's school that had photographs of HODs and teachers stapled to it. Except this was weather-worn, and the photographs were of sponsors and staff, arranged according to neither rank nor contribution. Perhaps by age or nationality—but who could tell? The faces taped to the lopsided board were mostly grey and blurry, some were identifiable only by the names inscribed on the stickers stuck below them. Cheryl spotted Juwel almost immediately. Farther down the row was a beaming Vikash.

Skipping to the third row of photographs, she fixed her eyes on the fifth face from the left. What bright eyes! What a smile! The woman had beautiful round eyes, accentuated by her defined eyelids. The life in those eyes could not be dimmed by the lousy quality of the photograph. Cheryl Dada tried to imagine a younger incarnation of the woman whose name was MADAM C— The rest of the name tag had fallen off, leaving behind a sticky residue of glue that trapped dust and flies. In her mind Cheryl Dada was colouring the woman's grey fraying hair black and ruffling the unfashionable backswept bob. Looks aren't everything, but surely one must have colour!

She strolled over to the other side of the greenhouse, stopping by the pond. The goldfish were swimming in circles, their mouths puckering at the surface of the water, as if coming up for a breather.

"You and I both," Cheryl Dada said to the fish. She could still see herself playing with the carps, dipping her hands into the pond in Bishan Park. She used to go there with her mother to take pictures. She would watch the fish swim and turtles climb to the rocks while her mother walked around with her clunky Rollei camera, searching for pretty sights and interesting people to photograph. Sometimes she would come by the pond where Cheryl was and take pictures of children dipping their feet in the pond or feeding the white and orange fish. There was this one time, Cheryl remembered in detail, when her mother stood on the bridge and watched her and some kids play by the pond. Later, when everyone was gone and they were packing up, her mother told her how beautiful the kids were and wished Cheryl were like them.

As a child she had frizzy hair that made her head look round, like a mushroom. Rebonding was not yet a thing in the '70s. Although Cheryl was slender, baby fat accumulated in her cheeks, causing her tiny face to puff up at the sides. Her primary school friends called her Pau because of her round face—the nickname stuck with her through her adolescent years. Even when she lost the baby fat, revealing her naturally high cheekbones and thin jaw, she was still conscious of her fat face. She always deprecated her fleshy cheeks, which seemed to her too prominent for her personality, singling her out as the pau face when she'd rather be obscure. To her friends, to her mother, she was still that pau face. To herself, she was always ugly. Even she would not want to get chummy with a kid like that.

Turning around to head back to the front of the greenhouse, Cheryl Dada approached the door once more. She paused to look again at the furry board. This time her eyes rested briefly on the photograph beside Madam C's: it featured a darker-skinned man with a rectangular face. It was not clear if he had stubble or if it was the poor grainy quality of the photograph, but the specks made him look bristly and unkempt. If there was anything she disliked in a man, it was a beard. Irked by the face, Cheryl Dada rolled her eyes and wandered over to the next photograph.

Her concentration was interrupted by a stubborn rhythmic beep. It drew her gaze to the Casio watch on her wrist. It was precisely three.

"Three!" she said. "My God, it's three." Cheryl Dada was alarmed by the number on her watch. The party! The party! She must stop dallying. She reached for the door handle and turned it.

There they were! Lilies! White lilies!

VI

What is he looking at? Cheryl Dada thought as she opened the door and saw the man sitting in the guest room.

She was not in the mood to play host, not after all that toiling in the sun. Cautiously, she approached the sofa, hoping he would not speak to her. Her arms were feeling the ache from carrying the flowers and her chiffon top was still wet from the jaunt. Cheryl Dada thought she could have some time alone and enjoy the cool air in the guest room. She wanted badly for the man to go away but he kept looking at her. Did she have pollen on her face?

"How are you?" said the man.

Do I know him? thought Cheryl Dada, trying to put a name to the ruddy face. The watch beeped twice; it brought no name to her. She was getting impatient and looked over to the man, willing him to leave. He looked uneasily back at her. His lips parted slightly to take a breath; he was about to speak.

If he knows me, then I must know him, thought Cheryl Dada, as her watch beeped again and failed to derail her cycle of thoughts. But from where? Certainly not from here—there were no male residents. Where do I know him from? she asked again, her eyes preoccupied with a head-to-

toe inventory of the man sitting on the sofa. The thicket of dark curls; the stubble; the left dimple; the strong jaw; the silver chain that wore no pendant; the red and blue checked shirt with stiff collar; the faded jeans; the unpolished and dusty boots; the faint lilt in the voice—

"I'm Adam," he said, his voice slightly trembling. She's the same, he thought, rising from the sofa and stretching his hand out to her. His beeping watch said hello on his behalf.

Cheryl was hesitant but shook the hand anyway, for she lacked the will to refuse. Formalities caught her off guard. Moreover, she thought she must know the man; she just could not yet remember exactly who he was and where she had seen him. She had no choice but to settle down beside him—the close proximity might jolt a memory.

They sat quietly in the room. There were two large windows, two empty bookshelves, and the worn out sofa. On the coffee table was a copy of yesterday's *Straits Times* and the Bible. The air conditioner made a whirring sound that filled the space between them.

"Busy day, huh?" he said.

"Everybody's so busy. The staff are running around, and meanwhile, residents are just resting in their rooms. I mean, I would too, knowing how crazy tonight will be," he laughed softly. "That's why I'm here—chilling in the guestroom. You too, right? Stealing some alone time and enjoying the air-con. Gosh, it's such a hot day. And they say there is no global warming. Isn't it obvious that world temperatures are rising?"

The question ushered in a series of news reports and *National Geographic* stories about sea levels and Singapore's low-lying East Coast, the $1.2 billion that would be pumped into improving the country's drainage system—"We can't have that whopping one metre of rainfall again. Orchard Road would shut down!" he said, "One week it is raining cats and dogs, the next it is blistering hot. Do you know the average temperature for the whole of last week was thirty-two degrees?"; at this point, he took a handkerchief from his pocket to wipe the sweat on his forehead and said, "Do you mind if I blast the air-con some more?"

The air conditioner was cranked up.

Cheryl turned to peruse the man who had just recited his monologue. He was a disastrous blend of a weather pundit, civil servant and Captain Planet. Before he could notice, she looked down at her white Birkenstock sandals, discomfited.

"Today is way too hot. It must be thirty, at least."

"Thirty-four." Cheryl readily said her line, pleased to release the information that was at her fingertips.

Adam smiled. "Woah, really? That is ridiculous. How did Singapore get so hot?" he said with unconvincing frustration.

"Tomorrow will be thirty-four too," she said. "Too fucking hot."

"Too fucking hot, indeed," he said in a lilting voice that betrayed his delight. "I wonder if the air-con is escaping, and that's why it is so stuffy in here. Maybe the door is not shut properly." He got up and walked to the door.

Cheryl raised her head to see him open and shut the door a few times. Then he patted the door, relaxed his grip on the knob and walked back to the sofa.

"Well, it's not the door. Glad to report that the door is a high functioning door, as tightly shut as can be." Encouraged by her responsiveness, or the lack of hostility, he carried on, "The door is functioning better than the air-con."

His companion sniffed, which was better than a snicker. He was more encouraged than ever and decided to catch the wave of her interest.

"Do you remember," he said, "the doors in MPH?"

"My God, they were fucking heavy," she replied almost instinctively; and she recalled the towering glass doors with wooden panels. They had bruised her arm once.

"Yes they were," he said, on cue. They hurt me too, he wanted to add, but halted the words flooding his mind. He would sound too emotional, he would give away too much. He had learned from past experiences that intimate talks did not work as well as rambling soliloquys—which threw her off and made it difficult to form hasty conclusions, giving her more time to warm up to his presence.

"Why did they have to make them so heavy?" she said, permitting her aching body to relax in the sofa.

"Exactly," he said. "How strong does one need to be to enter a bookstore?"

Cheryl, catching on, began to laugh; Adam laughed too.

Promptly the room expanded. The shelves were lined with books; the doors became weighty. There they were in the old MPH on Stamford Road: Adam behind the cashier and Cheryl queuing to pay for her book. When it was her turn, she pulled out from her cloth purse two crumpled one-dollar notes. One of them had a tear in the middle. He was at first hesitant to receive the money from her, for the store manager had just a few hours earlier briefed the new recruits to decline torn or pasted-together notes with tact and courtesy—"Remember to ask customers if they got other notes. Say we cannot accept torn ones. Say the bank don't want to accept also." But when Adam saw her soft doe eyes, helpless and tentative, as if on the verge of tears, he forgot the instructions and told her it was all right. She blushed; those eyes glowed with a hope that he alone had given her.

He wanted to assure her again as he always did. He wanted to tell her that everything was going to be all right. That he would be with her; that he was waiting for her to get well. Yes, they were older, and things had changed over the past few years. Yes, they were living apart—oh how he hated sleeping alone!—but it was common these days, wasn't it? People in other countries get separated all the time, Adam reasoned to himself, thinking of his cousin Sonia, who had gone to Manchester to do a Ph.D. while her husband stayed behind and continued with his job at some medical college. Two-year-old Ayesha went along with her mother and refused to speak Urdu after that.

"Who ask him to let her go study?" "Who ask him to sign the prenup?" Tongues were wagging, wagging outside

Pakistan. Adam remembered that his father had a lot to say about Sonia's decision. His mother too. But the crux of the matter, which everyone seemed to have missed, was Yasir had stayed behind in Lahore. Yasir stayed behind; he waited faithfully. He could not just pack up and leave, especially when his folks were old and sick. More importantly, there was no need for them to be in the same place because the separation was temporary. Sonia was going to come back—where else could she go? He knew for a fact she was coming back. He had to believe that. And Yasir believed right because Sonia came back four years later and they moved to Islamabad. Distance had not done anything to the marriage.

People should think less of distance, Adam thought, stealing a glance at the fair hand that was reaching for the newspaper on the table. Long-distance is nothing, he thought. Although, how would we know that when we are spoiled by the luxury of spatial constraints? We don't know what long-distance is, he lamented to himself; we don't know what longing is. Two points are enough to establish distance, just like two people are enough to make love. They think they're happy, he said to himself, looking briefly at the two smiling faces on the newspaper that had entered his view: "Sixteen-hour labour for local celebrity Odessa Lee with no painkillers", which didn't seem like a big deal to him. The baby knows better, he thought, its face cringing in agony, as if it had been advised of the barbarous truth of life.

"The first-time parents say that they are relishing the arrival of their—" The page turned and the newspaper was back on the table. Adam had seen enough to know where the story was going. The young celebrities believed that their family was complete, that it was the best thing that would ever happen; motherhood or fatherhood or parenthood, it changed their lives. They're too young to understand, he thought and shook his head. Actually, most people in this country regardless of age only understand one kind of family.

But ours is a new kind of family, he said with a new confidence, trying to remember the show that Clare used to watch. The trailblazer kind of family. Mixed-race and religion-free. Nobody but themselves would understand this. It's no longer the '80s. Or the '90s. The 21st century is a whole new world.

"Modern Family," he mouthed the words as they came together in his mind. His family was modern, indeed—it was nothing like the one his parents had given him, and he had learned to stop comparing one with the other. Ice cream at Swensen's did not excite anyone. Family Sunday wasn't a thing. Coming home for dinner wasn't either. This was especially true after Clare had started university. The first year she stayed in hostel so her absence was reasonable; but when the absence became a norm, Adam tried to make weekend dinners a family tradition so that they could spend quality time together. In hindsight, he should have enforced this when Clare was much younger so she would understand the importance of having a real and loving family.

It was one thing to be a modern family, another thing to be incomplete. Even the most modern of families must have a father figure, a mother figure and children, though some choose to have pet dogs and cats instead. The point is—and Adam had always believed in this—the family has a natural order and one must respect nature. To mix everything up, roles and responsibilities jumbled together until the point where the family becomes single-parent... How cruel! Adam thought. How cruel to deprive a child of paternal love! What would people think? What would she think about her father—a freelance journalist whose hobbies were travelling, organic farming and surfing—he even said he liked surf music, what nonsense was that?—a man who made the cut because he wrote an essay on some women's march?

Adam had deleted the screenshots of the profile that Clare had sent him, but the details of the donor, which seemed unreal and cartoonish, were seared in his mind: "I hopped onto the Trans-Siberian from Moscow to Beijing with a ukulele and a Swiss Army knife," wrote Donor Number 523HEI; the personal statement was accompanied by a photograph of a grey-eyed baby boy who had a dimple in the chin. The whole process was a farce and Clare was sucked into the vortex of it. But there was no use trying to talk sense into her; she would only go on and on with her theories about women and the patriarchy. She would not listen and Adam would not listen too; they had stopped talking for years. Adam did not reply to her messages and he did not attend the baby shower. He stopped trying. The baby girl, the baby named Cheryl, was a stranger to him. For no Dada ever had a dimple in their chin.

Adam noticed his thoughts and stopped. An unexpressed emotion gushed up from inside him. His mind was spinning. How had things between Clare and him deteriorated so rapidly over the years? He considered himself to be liberal and open-minded as long as no one was hurt in the name of freedom. But now, a baby was involved. Was she ready for the world? Was the 21st century ready for her?

Just then, as the questions turned over in his head, Adam understood that modern meant different things to him and to Clare. He was modern for his time but nowhere modern enough for her. There is a limit to how modern a person can be.

Adam was modern in his own right. He would come home early to do the house chores, wash and iron the clothes, put up the Chinese New Year and Eid decorations and tear them down after the festivities, send Clare to school and ensure that everyone was fed. Most important to him were the family dinners. He would cook, even though his pilaf was not as fluffy as his mother's and the raita lacked punch. The food was always missing something because he was haphazard about proportions. He thought if Martin Yan could pinch salt and toss whatever amount into the pot, he could too. Questions of how much or how little, how many grams and how many teaspoons, Adam did not care for.

Needless to say, there were always leftovers at the table. Much food and money were wasted in those few years. They ate so little: the younger one would peck at the yellow rice; the older one would fish out the spices and chili seeds. His mother had taught him to leave nothing behind on the plate, that one must not waste food; Adam wanted to impart the same values to his daughter, but it was hard to set an example when Cheryl left those seeds and pods and whatnots on the plate, stalks of vegetables lying on the table.

After his mother-in-law's death, the dinner situation exacerbated. Some nights the plates of food would go untouched. In those months Cheryl grew thin. It wasn't just the pale cheeks and thin neck, or the increasingly defined collarbones. Her gait was slow and stiff and she had become hesitant in her ways. Adam would find her hands clasping a cup, occasionally raised to nearly touch her lips only to be brought back to rest on her lap. They repeated the dance over and over until the tea was cold, then there would be a new cup of steaming hot tea; and it began again: the hands, trembling, rising and falling; the white cloud swirling above the cup; the lips pursed, disturbing the surface of the tea, quivering as the sinuous threads of smoke blew upwards. When she was dazed like that, it was as if she had lapsed into a state of nonbeing where her body was anchored in the moment and the rest of her adrift on a sea of memories whose mighty waters engulfed the fragile present. Wave after wave they carried her farther away from him. Then she was lost on the shores of someplace out of reach. On his lucky days, he would find her in the attic, sitting in the rocking chair, glassy-eyed for hours. He would call out to her but it was clear to him that she was in a world of love that was not his.

It seemed strange to think that she would entertain a life without him, that they were ever without each other, that each was a self-sufficient person before this life of theirs together. For everything that had happened to him, everything that he thought mattered prior to meeting her—an Engineering degree, money, status and all the five Cs—turned out to be a series of empty and looping chases. In the beginning Cheryl wasn't there in his life and then all of a sudden, it was as if she had always already been there, as if he had never been without her.

Gradually, one day at a time, Cheryl weakened. Her emaciation outlasted the acceptable mourning period. It was a symptom of what Adam interpreted to be a midlife crisis. Such abnormal behaviour was called "acting out", just like how Clare was "acting out"—as her form teacher had put it to him—when she shaved off part of her hair in secondary school. His wife was acting out so as to regain control. It was the only logical explanation for her refusal to eat. He thought Cheryl was trying to get her slender form back—an attempt to recapture her youthful days—and she was succeeding. Her pyjamas were slipping off her shoulders and the ring on her finger was loose. For a while she became skinny as she had been in university. Then she got smaller—as if her skeletal frame had contracted and her waist were corseted. The true extent of the loss was revealed when even her elastic belt could not hold her jeans up any more. Her clothes no longer fit her and she had to wear Clare's old shirts like they were dresses.

Still Adam cooked on the weekends in hopes that what would entice the stomach could win the heart. Oh how Cheryl played with food, picking up the rice, grain by grain, with her chopsticks. He did not know how to put it across to her that it was rude and simply inefficient because she was holding the chopsticks the wrong way. "They aren't supposed to cross like that," he told her. "They should be parallel to each other," he told Clare. But no matter how hard he tried to show his girls, they were obdurate.

Cheryl eventually lost the desire and energy to finish anything, be it the rice on her plate or the part-time degree at SIM. She stopped coming to dinner, and Adam ate in silence with Clare who, like her mother, became very particular, only eating pastas and burgers and mostly Western food. (The Hawaiian pizza used to be her favourite. He tried to make that for her on her 12th birthday, kneading and rolling out his own pizza dough, adding sweet corn and red capsicum among the pineapples and tomatoes. But Clare spat them out, every single capsicum and corn. She said it was her worst birthday and from that day on hated Hawaiian pizza.) Family gatherings were often postponed because Cheryl was too tired to get out of bed. Their annual trip to Islamabad had to be cancelled and rescheduled twice or thrice before Adam gave up and went on his own. And there was that scarf that

Cheryl was always knitting. Whatever progress made in the morning was unpicked and left entangled on their bed at night; the fraying wool between them.

Adam adjusted himself in the sofa, thinking about how thin she used to be. Not to mention how this wretched place had aged her. More white hair, he noted the moment she entered the room. His wife had been neglected in the home, her hair dry and undyed. He must remember to bring more Brand's essence of chicken next time.

He rolled up his sleeves, and then unrolled them. She has put on some weight, he thought, slightly relieved. He raised his head to catch a view of her; Cheryl was busy examining her colourless nails. She is much better than when she first moved in, he thought, remembering how they had fought her decision to check herself into a home—a rare moment in the Dada history where father and daughter were in agreement. But Adam and Clare could not dispute the diagnosis that Cheryl was starving herself and struggling with some unnamed crisis. The doctor's recommendation was precise: a nursing home or rehab centre. Cheryl was more than cooperative to heed medical advice. Because rehab was temporary, she chose the home that she knew would not kick her out.

At least her mood is good today, Adam thought. Parties always lifted her spirits; all the prep work and bustle kept her occupied. At least she has the strength to walk on her own without the wheelchair, he thought. He must not forget that her being here, alive, was a miracle in itself.

As if sensing his gaze, Cheryl turned from him, looking in the direction of the outside light. He could almost hear her thinking that she must get away from him, that he was some lecherous man, that he was up to no good. (One time she had mistaken him for a police investigator and demanded that Daniel send him away. Another time she had bitten his hand, calling him a representative from Management.) They had been married for 30 years now... and to be treated like this...her back towards him... It was hurtful, utterly cruel! To be treated by the love of his life with such disrespect, coldness—he couldn't stand it, not after what he had sacrificed for her.

Cheryl did not turn around. She was almost remembering him; she had seen those deep-set eyes, the thick eyebrows before. Were they friends from university? Perhaps a very, very distant relative, or a husband of one? Cheryl wondered. Could they be— The thought scared her; the L-word half forming in her mind. But what was she afraid of? Think of the couple in the newspaper who just had a baby, she urged herself. Think of their smiles—that can't be scary!

To give unreservedly to a point where losing oneself is okay, where what is lost becomes an afterthought, where to experience a myriad of feelings—pain, anguish, sorrow, hurt, despair, longing—that is the primacy of being, our duty as human beings, isn't that Love? Or Life, all the same? Love is not scary; it cannot be. Love is love is love.

Love is really in the air, thought Cheryl Dada, admiring the view from the window: the tree branches formed an arch like a rainbow, the leaves wavering in the wind. Love is love is love, the words looped in her head. It seemed to her that in love the end has no end. Even Nature could not stop it.

Sitting close to the other end of the sofa, Adam shifted forwards, as if to listen to what she had to say. She was in another world, watching the birds and tree and clouds and whatnots. How can one lose oneself if Love builds us? he thought, crossing his legs. Love is—what was it she said? Love is commitment. Love is dedication. Love is action. Love is—was that it?—Love is love? How could she think it was so simple? If love is love, then what is love exactly? The question cannot answer itself. And that was exactly her problem: she would never say it because she did not have a clue what it was. Love is love, Adam scoffed, letting out a grunt.

But he was not like her; he wasn't a flake. He knew what it meant to love somebody. Love is a decision, an action. It is not talk; it cannot be just talk. When he decided to marry her, it was for life, regardless of what might happen in the future. That was love, wasn't it? There was nothing abstract or complicated about it. If love was something, it was action. Sure, it wasn't always easy, but it had to be done. And wasn't it clear to her that all these years he was always acting on his love for her? He wished she could do the same for him. Anyhow, nothing was going to change the way he felt about her. His love was a done deal, guaranteed and irrevocable. He especially wanted to tell her that.

If only he could recount to her the story of how they had met in the bookstore... It was a love against all odds! If only she could just sit for a moment and listen to him. It began in a bookstore... His father was Pakistani and his mother was Chinese. That he was Muslim did not seem to bother her. Even though she did not quite understand his culture—she had, like many others, mistaken him to be Indian—she received him with such openness that he was grateful and determined to marry her. Mrs Lee, however, was a different story. A fiercely legalistic Protestant, she detested him from the start, judging that he was a descendent of Ishmael. The fact that he was hairy did not help his case. Adam was set on changing her mind about that. He sent her flowers and planned fancy dinners. He shaved his face constantly, sustaining major razor burns, and took care to wear smart shirts, colourful checked shirts to distract her from focusing on his brownness. He even went to church with them every Sunday. But nothing convinced Mrs Lee of his sincerity. At his wits' end, Adam came close to committing apostasy, but he could not bring himself to sin against his father. After a year of turmoil, he was on the brink of depression, about to give up on true love.

It was Cheryl who held on to him. Despite her mother's objections, she continued to go out with him. She said that they did not need her blessing, that her mother was never going to be happy with whoever she went out with—Muslim or Catholic or Hindu. That she was only worried her place in heaven would be affected by her daughter's choice. She told him that her mother didn't really care about her so he should not care too much about what she thought of them either. Adam wanted to love her so badly that he let himself be persuaded that a mother could be selfish.

He would do anything for their love. And he was certain that Cheryl felt the same. She would sneak out of her house to meet him, often lying to her mother about her whereabouts. Because of him, she became defiant. That was proof of how much she wanted to be with him! She was even willing to forgo pork! His mother had told him that the Chinese took their roasted pork and char siew seriously. So Adam took her sacrifice to mean she was going to marry him with or without her mother's approval. She was changing her life for him! What luck! So in 1983 when the Mass Rapid Transit Corporation was assembling an engineering team, he jumped on board. Adam did well and rose quickly through the ranks, well enough to pay for Cheryl's dowry. Theirs was a star-crossed love. It wasn't arranged; it was pure romance. The whole thing had a novelistic quality.

Whenever he yearned for her, he would remember her with some book in her hand and the torn one-dollar note. Oh how she spoke so little and slowly, like an innocent, cautious girl who had been told by her mother that the world was a dangerous place and every man was an enemy. But she had let him in. She let him in!

Now, looking at her delicate skin, her thin lips glossed in red, Adam felt a stir in his loins. His face was turning red.

After all these years, after what life had put her through, she was still beautiful. There was an ethereal pink gleaming under the once-porcelain face.

He wanted to kiss her, to seize that chin and caress that face, to live their lives all over again. He longed for the girl in queue for the cashier and here she was sitting right beside him; yet he must not touch her.

Through the glass, Cheryl too saw herself standing in line. She seemed anxious, her hand pulling at her skirt. Even when it was her turn to pay, she was hesitant, looking to the cashier for assurance. She heard the clicks of the cash machine, the jingling of coins, the ruffling of plastic bags. And then the cashier said something and she turned red.

As she felt the rush of blood to her cheeks, the name came back to her. "Adam," the boy said. He said his name was Adam. Alas, it dawned on her that it was him—the boy at the cashier, the man in the guest room—they were the same person. The familiar face; the curls; the dimple on the left cheek; the olive brown skin. He was the boy, bigger and all grown up, but still the same. She saw him now. Adam; she remembered.

He caught a familiar tenderness in her eyes, a youthful reticence was possessing her. Her eyes were glinting.

"I've missed you," he said with a boyish smile, his voice thin and quivering. "I miss you," he tried again.

I know, she wanted to say.

Both were trying, both remembering. They had returned to each other; the girl and boy in the bookstore.

"Cheryl, my darling!" he let out without restraint, tearing up.

"Cheryl, Cheryl!" he cried out to her, fighting the want to hold her thin frame in his arms.

"Do you remember me?" he pleaded. "Do you?" His voice was almost breaking.

Her eyes were watery too. She did not have to say a word; he knew she was back. Here she was—at last—sane! Back in his life!

Now that she was facing him, he could behold her face without shame. "My love," he said, not shifting his eyes from her. "Happy birthday, dear." To his words, she gave a faint smile. The lines near her eyes gave away the time spent in this godforsaken place; they made her look weary and wasted.

But they're also marks of wisdom, Adam quickly consoled himself, recovering in a split second. ("You've either a degree in optimism or oblivion," his daughter had said to him.) "Lines of wisdom," he repeated in his mind. His wife was a person who thought deeply and excessively about people, the sagacious type who brooded too much for her own good. Always in the mood for thought, she was tormented by depressive ruminations, which made her more prone to... Adam paused to find the word. She...she is more prone to— No, no, no! These were Dr Pitts's words! Why was he parroting him? Adam castigated himself for thinking like the doctor and was filled with shame. No! How could he think that! She was his wife! It wasn't that she thought too much (Dr Pitts was wrong this time!), she just thought too highly of the world and its lodgers. Her heart was too big for the world. She thought it could fill her but not even two earths and all the oceans would quench her want. Adam, knowing that no content would fill her, tried to tame the heart. Great love was meant to be given; he took it upon himself to help her spread the love. He saw in her what she herself did not know: she would be the perfect wife, the perfect mother to their children.

At first he was unsure about how she would feel about marrying him. There were too many obstacles: her mother, their religions, the six-year age gap. His mother told him not to rush and that marriage was not always the first thing on the minds of new age girls like Cheryl. Adam was torn: he could not wait to propose to her but agreed that his mother had a point. He went back and forth, entreating God for signs and imagining the possible outcomes, thinking he might hold off the thought until after her studies. Then, as if his diligent prayers had paid off, and they were destined to be together, all the weeks of fretting and agonising were suddenly relieved after a telephone call from Cheryl. She had rung him from Mount Alvernia and was sobbing. He thought he had heard wrongly because her voice was quavering. He waited on the line until she calmed down; then she said: "Seven weeks." She was seven weeks pregnant.

It was the best news. Now, Cheryl would say yes to him. Even her mother would have to oblige. He did not have to hesitate any more. For Adam—and this was the truth of the matter—all his life—and he had difficulty admitting this to himself—was terrified of rejection. It was for this reason that he never asked Cheryl how she felt about the pregnancy or if she was happy about it, because what if she wasn't?

Fondling the ring that wrapped his finger, Adam felt some scratches. Their marriage had taken some hits and this was another storm. But like the ones before, they would get through this together. They did, after all, manage to coax her mother to attend the wedding—which was one of the toughest battles he had to fight. Only on the account of her granddaughter and a 10-course Chinese banquet at Shangri-La Hotel did she agree to show up. They were triumphant because they stayed together. That's what married couples do in the face of trouble. His parents had set a good example for him. His mother had run away from her family to be with her father; his father had never left his mother, even when she became bedridden, a consequence of terminal lymphoma. Until the end he was with her, holding her, assuring her of their love.

Adam's father hated the cancer as much as he loved his wife; and since it was part of her, he learned to love it too. In him Adam saw what love looked like. He promised to be true to Cheryl in good times and in bad, for better or for worse, in sickness and in health. He promised he would love her and honour her all the days of his life. Today was no different.

Through it all, Adam was thankful for Cheryl. He believed she was thankful for him too. For one moment, absentmindedly, he relaxed and leaned back.

"I love you"—the words gyred, and hovered above them. She made no comment, but he understood that expression was not her strength. He moved slightly towards her; she was composed; the clock on the wall was ticking. Then, seizing the moment of intimacy, finally casting aside his fear of rejection, Adam rested his hand on her thigh and stroked her gently.

Feeling his hand on her, Cheryl stiffened. She looked fixedly at the unmasculine fingers that were gripping her skin.

"Come to my party," she said in a toneless voice, reeling in the invisible line that joined their memories.

Adam roused from his stupor. "Of course," he said, shifting himself away from her along the sofa. As if he, too, were aware that the room was shrinking.

VII

Mrs Dada woke up to a light knock on the door.

"Hello, Mrs Dada," said Daniel, hesitant to enter the guest room. "Is this a bad time?"

"Come in." She yawned, moving herself to the edge of the sofa.

"Sorry, did I wake you?"

"It's all right," she said, rubbing her eyes, "I must have dozed off."

"Cheok said you're looking for me?"

"Yes. I want to know the seating arrangement for tonight," said Cheryl Dada, in what she thought was a commanding tone. "Have you got that sorted out?"

"Yes, I have. Your table is somewhere in the middle—"

"Who is coming?" she cut in. "Who's on the guest list? Do you have the full list with you?"

"I—"

"Who's at my table?" persisted Cheryl Dada.

"I don't have it with me."

"How come?"

"It's on my desk," said Daniel. He cleared his throat.

"Do you know who's sitting at my table?" she asked again.

"I don't know that yet. But I will as soon as I go back to

the office," said Daniel, keeping his eyes on her slightly ruffled hair.

She's getting on, he thought to himself, especially of late. Still, he thought, she had a prominent face; the strong cheekbones gave her a natural dignity. The face of Mrs Dada with wisps of grey and white hair reminded Daniel of Bai Fa Mo Nu. She wasn't old too, just heartbroken. Ling Qing Xia's hair turned white overnight because she had been betrayed by Leslie Cheung. Mrs Dada was just as belligerent—a virago in her own right. Maybe she was hurt by love too. But her husband seemed nice and patient; he was one of those hopeful family members. Mr Dada came thrice a week—whether Mrs Dada wanted to see him or not was a different thing. The daughter visited often too, though her visits had been getting sporadic the last couple of months—Lulu mentioned that she was travelling to Canada a lot. Apparently she was busy with the visa application and sorting out some housing matters.

Mrs Dada seems to have a loving family, Daniel thought, trying to recall the last time he had seen the three of them together, but could not remember anything concrete. The real story of Cheryl Dada was not in her files. Rather than a family issue, he wondered if the reason why she was here was because she thought too much about things and just would not let them go. Overthinking and stress can cause hair to turn white prematurely, as does smoking. Some residents were like that: they smoked too much and hung on for nothing, making life harder for themselves. Some of them, as they stayed longer, lost faith and hope and, sitting in their wheelchairs, reran the pages of their lives and tried to cancel every mistake they could find, to descend gradually into madness. Might this be the decompensation that Dr Pitts was talking about?

"You cannot remember who's at my table?" The loud voice spiralled over his head and broke his train of thought.

"Not at the moment, but I will check and get back to you," Daniel said, remaining somewhat calm. "I know Adam is coming; I just saw him. Clare—"

"She's not coming."

"Okay."

"So did you get the drinks?" said Cheryl Dada, looking at him.

Daniel threw her a perplexed look; then said yes. That he would get it later.

"So you didn't..." she said, with an elevation of the eyebrows.

"No. I had to go somewhere so—"

"Oh. I thought you went out with Yu Yu to get the drinks..." said Cheryl, searching his eyes. She spoke slowly so that the words sounded less interrogative.

But his eyes shifted to avoid hers.

Cheryl caught the expression. Then she knew, as he knew too.

A long pause settled in the room.

After a bit he said in a measured tone: "I'll get them right after this."

"Remember to come back and tell me who's at my table," she said.

"Yes, I will."

"Don't forget again," she added.

"I won't." He blinked, and took a step back, almost turning around to leave. Then, recalling his errand, he stopped and said to her: "Oh, there's a letter for you that came in this morning."

His casual tone was an attempt to hide his nervousness, for the postman did not deliver on public holidays. He had meant to pass the letter to her yesterday but it completely slipped his mind. He also forgot to inform her about Mr Dada's visit and forgot to get the drinks. The one thing on Daniel's mind was ousting the rest of his thoughts, the things on his to-do list, the events on his calendar; but it would be over soon, after today his life would change. All things led up to this evening. He would do it in the herb garden, knowing Yu Yu relished the smell of rosemary. With fireworks in the sky, he would go down on his knees and Lucky would scamper out, the ring tied to his collar. It was going to be a romantic night.

"What letter?" Cheryl Dada asked, annoyed by his foolish grin.

"This one," Daniel replied, quickly retrieving a brown envelope from his back pocket. "I'll leave it here," he said, sidling back into the room and placing it on the coffee table.

"I'll get the drinks and let you know the seating arrangement as soon as I get back," said Daniel, trying to back up and leave the room and its occupant.

"I won't forget this time."

"You'd better not."

"Yes, Ma'am. I'll see you later, Mrs Dada," he said quickly, walking out and closing the door behind him.

Alone again, Cheryl remembered Cheok's words: "They very gum you know?" Did he mean tight? Sticky? Like siblings? Thick as thieves? Or did he mean—

Cheryl stopped her thoughts. They very gum, she repeated silently in her head. But was it really that? The thought was ludicrous to her.

But one must try feeling now. If it feels right to them, then go for it. If colour did not matter, why should nationality? Or age? Or gender? And language issues were secondary. The home had taught her that gestures could make up for speech impairments. Unless one were physically impaired, of course. A few things could stop the heart from wanting: a stroke being one of them. Most of the time the heart wants and keeps on wanting. "Feeling, feeling, feeling," said Cheryl Dada, repeating her life's motto to the rhythm of the beeping that came from no direction. One must feel, feel, feel—

At the last beep of the watch, her concentration broke and Cheryl Dada remembered her party. It was already five—she must go back and change.

Making her way to the door, Cheryl noticed the brown envelope that was sitting on the table. She picked it up and lifted it to the light, trying to peer through the paper.

"To Lee Chia Le," she read, dragging her fingers over the curlicue words in blue, feeling the dents on the envelope, and tracing the pen strokes. The name was strange to her as the address on the back.

"The Beeches... Cardigan Road..." Cheryl murmured the words slowly, relishing each syllabus, "Marlborough... Wiltshire..." They were like stars twinkling, confusing but wondrous, like some beautiful nonsense taken from one of Roald Dahl's books. But nobody she knew lived in the UK.

Just then the sun began to illuminate the room; beams of light entered through the shut windows, unfurling across the marble floor, as if privy to the contents of the letter. Cheryl carefully tore along the edge of the envelope and pulled out a pastel blue card.

Dear Le,

I hope you haven't forgotten me because I think of you every 9 August. Remember the poem we read about the world being mud-luscious and puddle-wonderful? Now that I'm older, I see it. Do you?

I hope you're having a smashing day. I hope many good things for you. Happy birthday, human bean!

scrumdiddlyumptiously,
Sarah

The name tugged at her heart; she blushed, rested against the door, and for a moment felt a youthful energy return to her. Cheryl had thought of her too. She remembered the poem; every word of it. The little lame baloonman; the queer old baloonman. Balloon spelled wrongly. The baloonmen were far and wee, they were whistling. Cheryl remembered all of it. How could she forget? Even now, as she was sliding the card back into the jagged envelope, she was thinking of her.

Sarah was running, she was always running towards her. Cheryl saw her running to the gate behind the canteen. Her face was scarlet, she was panting. She said she was sorry she was late; that she had been given two demerit points for talking to Constance Tan in Maths class when she was only trying to help her pass a letter to Ruth Goh who was sitting behind her; that the teacher was a stupid bitch. Her face was forcing a smile, but petulance knitted her brows together.

"I wasn't talking," she said, "I swear I wasn't."
"How did she—"
"I was only whispering."
"Did Constance get a demerit point?"
"No."
"What did she—"
"I just passed the stupid message."

Her lips, Cheryl remembered, were pink and full, set into a natural pout that eased the sobriety of her thoughts. They were quivering as she drew deep breaths through her mouth. There the girls stood, face to face, Sarah still panting, her chest heaving; Cheryl was standing in the afternoon sun. They came close; closer.

In the room, Cheryl stiffened. She kept very still, worried a slight movement might let escape from her the memory that she ached to relive. She felt the strain in her neck, sweat streaking her lower back. It was a hot afternoon. It was still St Joan's.

In a moment of impulse, Cheryl reached to touch Sarah's face. She wanted to feel if it was as warm as it was red, but it wasn't. Embarrassed, she looked down at her shoes:

"I'm sorry, I was..." she mumbled; the words faded away.

"What?"

A pause.

"Say it, say it!"

Nothing was the reply. Cheryl kept her eyes cast down, and then watched as the other pair of shoes disappeared from her sight.

The memory slipped from her mind; her hand loosened its hold on the creased letter. Like a part removed, a phantom pain burned in her chest. Cheryl Dada looked round at the aching void of the room. She could feel it whirling, every moment of the day closing in on her. Hoping some open space would salve the strain of laboured breathing, Cheryl Dada grabbed the door knob.

But why now? Why this? she thought, stepping out of the room. She quickened her steps, walking as fast as her ailing legs could take her. Why was she missing what she barely knew? Did Sarah think about that too? They were 13, for goodness' sake! They knew nothing. They only felt tenderly for one another, their hearts clubbing away inside, her hand fast in hers, they hadn't realised that they needed a language for touch. How could they? How could they have known that light pecks and modest fondling between girls were the lust of the flesh? Like most kids, and adults too, they thought they had time to figure things out. When did they start losing time and how, so quickly? Cheryl stopped at the doors of the lift. Back then the world seemed so big, the world was hers and Sarah's. What they made of it was shared, and what they lost was doubled up.

Cheryl got into the lift and stood restlessly in the corner. The world, she thought, as the doors were closing, had become smaller as she got older. It narrowed into different tunnels, each tunnel boring its way into a set destination. The tunnels did not cross, and there was no turning back for anyone. She had taken one tunnel—and here she was. Sarah had taken another and ended up in London.

If only she had known better... If only she hadn't listened to her mother, who knew, she might be in London too. If-onlys were no good for her. John was quite right about that. Instead of thinking, she should be doing something about her thoughts. Journalling might help; filling up another one of those three-column table sheets might too. They would help her to "clear her mind" and "break the negative thinking pattern", according to the doctor. Yes, she decided that she would write to Sarah. She must write!

Thinking about this, Cheryl paced back and forth in the lift. She felt an urgent need to return to her room; she wanted to capture the thoughts before the questions departed from her. What is London like? Does it really rain all the time? Does Big Ben really strike every hour? Have you seen the Queen? The farthest place she had gone to was Islamabad—about nine hours away. Perth and Taipei tied for second place. Both were five hours away, give or take. She might go to Canada someday since Clare was moving there, probably a two-day flight or something. London, in comparison, seemed near—just a 14-hour flight away. Thinking in terms of hours made the distance less insurmountable. Sarah did not seem too out of reach like that.

Cheryl wanted to write to Sarah, beseech her to describe the world as it was supposed to be. Is London the world they dreamed of? Is life really greener on the other side? What exactly did this mud-luscious and puddle-wonderful world look like? For her life was not that. Not in the slightest. She thought of her crazy neighbours, Juwel, Vikash, Lulu, the healthcare staff, Management. She looked around at the shiny walls, the poster that was falling off: *JOIN US FOR KARAOKE NIGHT ON 1 AUGUST 2016!* The lift was making a wheezing sound. Cheryl felt a tightness in her throat. She was certain that this was not a wonderful world.

The lift doors opened and in walked Cheng Hong, holding a piece of drawing paper.

"Hello," said Cheryl.

"Hey, Cheryl," said Cheng Hong, her hand aiming for the door close button.

"Art class?" asked Cheryl, rubbing her nose.

"Nope. I just saw Pitts—he got me to draw my house," she said. Her finger was still pressing the button.

"Oh. He makes me draw too," said Cheryl.

"Draw what?"

"People, flowers, stuff. Once I drew a house."

"Yah, me too. I told him I can't draw. But he said never mind, it's just an exercise. I asked him which house to draw and he said anything. So I drew my attap house. You got live in one of those last time?"

"No. I don't remember. We were relocated to Toa Payoh."

"I remember a bit. But aiya, I anyhow draw. He also won't know what is kampong."

Cheryl chuckled. Cheng Hong held out the drawing for her.

"See, ugly right? I don't understand why he always makes me draw. Last week was flowers. The week before, I think, was what I like to eat."

It was a simple drawing in crayon; a pointed roof over a square. A house for a stick man.

"I'm not a drawer lah," Cheng Hong told her, as she tucked the paper under her arm. "I'm a cutter."

The lift doors opened again; there was no one. Both women reached for the door close button and their fingers touched briefly.

"Sorry," said Cheng Hong, withdrawing her arm.

Cheryl nodded abstractedly. Me too, she thought. "Me too."

She rehearsed over and over in her mind the words that would erase the distance between them. As if she could, on Cheng Hong's behalf, erase the lines on her wrist.

Cheng Hong understood without her saying anything. They were of the same kind, standing in the lift; both were haunted by the life outside its doors; the lines of age and love graven on their skin.

The lift came to a halt at the highest floor. The women barely moved.

"You first," said Cheng Hong, gesturing to the doors.

"Thanks," said Cheryl.

Without a parting word they exited the lift. Cheng Hong turned right and Cheryl went into the adjoining corridor.

VIII

Mrs Dada walked along the corridor, thinking about Cheng Hong. The jasmine notes of her perfume followed after her. Strange to feel like she knew her even though they hardly talked. Strange, Cheryl Dada thought, to feel that Cheng Hong knew her too, that she did not have to explain herself. They were not friends, just neighbours who had a dependence by virtue of being in the same place, alike in their afflictions. Like the verso and recto of a coin, they shared the currency that was—as John Pitts put it—stress. But perhaps what it really was was the lack of familiarity that enabled them to be conjoined without the burden of giving, of feeling too much for each other; theirs was a connection without the promise of a relationship. What is this strange mutuality of feelings? Cheryl Dada thought, her eyes surveyed the opposite block, the red and white streamers moving regally in the wind. Whatever it was, it refused to die away.

The feeling of being with a woman comforted Cheryl. She paused and leaned over the balustrade, feeling the breeze on the fifth floor. It was a nice feeling, nice to be alone together, understood but left unbothered. A more noble feeling than being married, tied to a husband, a child, a grandchild. It was a teaser of freedom, of what it might feel like to be unglued—the feeling of release, this being taken out of all the moulds that were fitted to her figure. Here, on the topmost floor, Cheryl Dada was above roles. Here, she was invisible.

She stretched out her arms to embrace the wind. At this time of the day the sun had mellowed and was retreating over the neighbouring block. That was block C. C for Cherry. It was the only residential block in the home that had an additional handrail mounted on the parapet wall of the second floor in memory of the beloved Yap Choon Eng. The ghastly bar, which doubled as a protective barrier, would have been an eyesore if not for the quasi-flowers painted in shades of pink and purple, thanks to Yu Yu, who had decided it was a great idea to get the still-life painting class to decorate the home. "To foster a sense of belonging," she explained to them. Daniel chimed in; it was something about unity in adversity. The rationale was rubbish but everyone appreciated the distraction. Even those who were not in the class participated, slapping paint on the railing with their bare hands. Cheryl's handprint was near the stairwell; it was the colour of periwinkle, Choon Eng's favourite flower.

Cheryl Dada turned away. She looked up to the sky that was filling up with clouds. Finally, it was getting cool. Tonight will be cool. What a perfect weather for a party, she thought. "Smashing weather! Smashing party! The party will be smashing!" Cheryl uttered excitedly, like a child trying to retain a newly learned word.

She let her elbows rest on the railing and peered down at the four women playing mahjong on the patio. There was Siew Eng (Cheryl recognised her over-permed hair); Felicia and her distinct hunch; Loudspeaker Leow—her real name was Leow Mei Ling—was shouting "Pong! Pong!" as she slammed the tile on the table. The fourth woman was unfamiliar. She had grey, medium-length hair and was wearing a shawl over her shoulder. There was something about her—obliqueness in her figure, blurriness of her face. Cheryl had a sudden urge to find out who she was. She wanted to rush down, take the stairs if she had to, to see her face. In her mind she was already there; but her legs would not take her. All she could figure out from where she was standing was that the woman was Chinese.

Downstairs, on the patio, the women's arms kept reaching forth to the middle of the table, one after the other, swiftly, never bumping into one another. A lot like hungry hippos chomping marbles, Cheryl thought amusedly. Each one extending forwards but never ever touching the other. She found the game ridiculous, an absolute waste of time—a bunch of silly hippos sticking their heads out for marbles. "For what?" Cheryl would ask. "Winner gets most marbles!" Adam said. And Cheryl would try again: "I mean for what?" "For the marbles!" he said. So they wasted hours on marbles. The game demanded no strategy or dexterity. Only fast fingers required. Nothing about it was educational. Cheryl much preferred Clare to play masak masak. She'd rather buy books and colouring sets. But it was his money so Adam bought whatever he wanted. He later got another set of Hungry Hungry Hippos because one hippo head had been dislodged. It was Rosie; Adam called the pink hippo Rosie. Though he was older, Cheryl seemed to have caught up with him, and Clare might have too.

Siew Eng, Felicia, Loudspeaker Leow and the mystery woman were mostly quiet, except for the occasional "pong" and "chi". The game looked synchronised and civilised from afar, but Cheryl was very familiar with the way of the game. She knew that underlying the seeming order was an unspoken urgency. "Faster lah," her mother used to say to the other aunties. "Why you so slow?" she would say impatiently. Sometimes she'd switch it up: "Fai di, fai di!" or "Ka kin lah!" depending on who the other players were. Some days when the table was filled with Hokkien aunties, Cheryl would not be able to understand a single word they said.

Although she was a bystander, Cheryl felt the anxiety at the table. She had to be extremely alert, listening out for cues so that she would know when to go and buy food. When it was the third hand—she had trained herself to note the shuffle and the change in feng—she would rush to the market across the road and dabao food so that the packed dinner would arrive home warm and ready to eat when they were done after a full game.

It was nerve-racking for her when she was just a kid buying food from the lecherous uncle at the noodle cart.

The way he said "Ah Muei", his inflection, the greasy hair. How he played with the ladle in his hand, the whistling and *kok kok kok* rippling behind her as she scurried away.

The sound of mahjong tiles shuffling was like thunder claps. The four women at the table had a different rhythm. Though the arranging of tiles was fast, the actual playing was moderate. It wasn't competitive, unlike her mother's games. There was no rush to win. This made sense to Cheryl, considering the fact that no real money was involved. They were most probably betting on cigarettes. Cheryl considered the other possible bets: a better seat at tonight's party, microphone privileges, choice of television programme to watch, an extra bowl of dessert, then decided that cigarettes made more sense. Of course the prize had to be the most destructive one.

The currency was different in the home. Worth was subjective, changing from day to day. If dinner was awful, then whoever had a storehouse of food was the winner. Once it was Oi Leng who possessed power because she had half a dozen of kueh lapis from Bengawan Solo that she exchanged for Milo and white coffee packets. Another time Cheryl had the upper hand because she had kept the box of maple shortbread Clare had bought for her from Canada.

Money wasn't valuable to the women. Not in a direct way. Even if it were of importance, most people preferred shillings. A $10 note was useless if they wanted to get something from the vending machine. Even $50 could not get them a drink. Nescafé and Yeo's did not accept notes and five-cent coins. Besides, having notes would mean asking a favour from someone for change. And favour would beget another favour. It was too much trouble for a canned drink.

Cheryl smiled to herself, finding her thoughts interrupted helpfully by a memory of Mama and her collection of one-cent coins; the old woman diligently depositing them one by one into the red pig, saving the rusty bronze as if it were gold. She would have been enraged knowing those were obsolete now, like banana money.

"Pong," shouted Loudspeaker Leow; her voice darted to Cheryl and dispersed the fragments gathering in her mind. She grabbed a tile from the mystery woman, and there was laughter. The woman with the dark brown shawl was blocked by Siew Eng, who was restless in her wheelchair, her body rocking back and forth. They handed out chips to Loudspeaker Leow, who quickly swept them into her drawer.

She could very well be called Eagle Leow too, since Mei Ling had eyes like a hawk, seeming to always get what she wanted. A real foodie, she was unscrupulous when it came to food. Mahjong was a means to the real prize; cigarettes were mere bargaining chips. When she won the game, she exchanged biscuits and kueh with the winnings. When she lost, she gave up the names of those who won the cigarettes to the nurses in exchange for some cereal and raisins. Either way, Mei Ling always won.

What's the exchange rate now? thought Cheryl, as she scrutinised the mess on the table. It used to be five blue chips and three green chips for a cigarette packet, or one yellow chip for a single stick. Cheryl moved slightly to the left and tiptoed to lean forwards.

Finally, as Siew Eng bent over to grab a runaway chip on the floor, Cheryl had a better view and caught a glimpse of the mystery woman's face.

"Ah!" cried Cheryl, squinting her eyes. What was she doing here? They had finally let her out. Being cooped up in the room was not going to make anyone feel better.

The woman waved her hand. And it was a strong hand. Definitely not ill, Cheryl thought, lifting her hand high in the air to say hi.

Suddenly, from the firmament, came a low roaring that drowned out her thoughts. Cheryl looked up; the women did too. Out of the white puffy clouds emerged a fleet of fighter planes.

"Oi, everybody come and see!" a woman dressed in red from the opposite building shouted to another resident who was stepping out of her room. "Eh quick come and see!" said another woman. The corridor was suddenly crowded; people squeezed in between people, heads were bouncing up and down as women tiptoed and fell back on their heels.

The first plane in line—it had a pointy nose—streaked across the sky, leaving a stream of thick white smoke. ("Wah, fighter jet leh!" hollered Loudspeaker Leow from the patio.) Two smaller planes followed its trail—Felicia steered her chair to the left, shouting, "Damn it! It's disappearing! Oh wait, got some more coming!"—and then two more fighter planes sliced through the sky. ("Wah!

Wah! Very fast leh!" said another. "Wait, I want to take picture—") They flew parallel to the horizon; contrails merging with the cumulous clouds. ("Wah lau, faster lah, going to no more already!") Then dipping slightly, one after another, the planes disappeared from the sky above them.

The moment after was quiet. The growling crowd, who had gathered in the corridor, was dismissed, the women heading back to their rooms. Downstairs, the four women withdrew to the table on the patio; the rectangular blocks of lifeless animals, flowers, bamboos, numbers awaiting them. Soon the hungry hippos were at it again.

Cheryl Dada watched the planes as they vanished, then turned away from the view of the sky, the table, the women.

It was almost time. The party was starting. She must change, she must leave now. So Cheryl Dada set off for her room, whisking through the corridor, blocking out the sounds of "pong" and "chi", of mahjong tiles knocking against the wooden table.

IX

At the door of room 5A was a red bag hanging from the doorknob. Cheryl Dada approached slowly. She extended her arm and pinched the bag by its strap. Examining the red tag tied to the zip, her shoulders relaxed and she allowed herself to bring the bag closer to her. The tag read—*51 NDP*. Well, it's about time, she thought, relieved that it had finally arrived. All week she had assumed the goodie bag would be the door gift at the party. She supposed this was a door gift too; but what was the party gift then? It had better not be something stupid like the travel adaptor. What were they thinking when they decided to purchase over a hundred adaptors for a bunch of women who went around in wheelchairs? Management had really outdone themselves with that last stint. Where did they think the residents were going?

Cheryl Dada rested her back against the door and rummaged through the contents of the bag: stickers of the flag and a big-eyed lion; a cap; a banner of some kind (too long to be a scarf, but maybe a table runner?); a packet of wet wipes; a plastic fan; some pamphlets and a colouring book (no crayons, she noted), a postcard and a brief historical write-up. She reached into the bag to search again. There was no Singa Lion. No Singa in red and white stripes, a camera slung around its neck. She had thought as much; the Jubilee year was over. What was she expecting anyway—a repeat of last year? But Cheryl Dada really wanted the Wally Lion. Perhaps even more than the baby who had taken it from her room. But she could not refuse a baby, especially a wailing one. And it was just a toy, for goodness' sake. Yet she found herself pining for the red, white and blue Singa. It was Wally; Wally had found his way to her. Cheryl had treated it as a token of her younger days; its absence made her think more about the past, about Clare, about the sense of her misdoings which had assailed her so often in recent months. She thought that perhaps if she had it again, it would ease her yearning for yesteryears, even if it were just standing there on the shelf, gathering dust.

Where's Wally was their thing—she and Clare. *Where's Wally? Where's Wally Now? Where's Wally in Hollywood? Where's Santa Wally? Where's Wally in Asia?* They had the whole collection of books. Instead of bedtime stories, Cheryl and Clare would spend half an hour or so searching for Wally before all the squinting and straining tired the little girl's eyes. To have Wally show up in her goodie bag last year was more than a pleasant surprise. To have found without searching, to be found when she thought all was lost, that had to mean something. Cheryl read it as a sign that she had done something right with Clare after all. And then she had to give Wally away without a fight.

For how can one say no to a baby? Cheryl revisited the thought, wondering about the power of babies. What was it about the tiny things that made even the toughest adult squirm? She was thinking of how Adam used to carry Clare in the wee hours of the night when she would not stop wailing, muttering gibberish while stroking her chin. Baby talk was just shrill tones, Adam whining on and on— *daa daa daa, oooh oooh oooh, goo goo goo, bah bah bah*. All that babbling and cooing woke her up. After the delivery, Cheryl only wanted a good sleep. Her body was aching for rest; her breasts were sore and she hated the stretch marks on her stomach, but the baby would not let up. She thought the birth was the hardest part but the worst was yet to come. No one warned her about the extent of a baby's appetite. The thing was a sucker; Cheryl had to wake up early in the morning and during the night to appease it. Adam tried to help, he really tried; but he was not the one with breasts. He did not have the maternal warmth that she was supposed to have. She read in a magazine that a baby recognises its mother's voice; she is the first to give it the gift of language, which is why it is called the Mother Tongue. As much as Adam wanted to give, Cheryl had to be the giver. Almost every day after the baby was born, Cheryl was dazed and irritable, on edge, surviving only on a couple of hours of disturbed sleep.

The most frustrating part was Cheryl could not understand what it wanted. She had heard people talk about the magical bond between mother and child but the only tangible connection, Cheryl felt, was when the baby sucked rapaciously from her nipple and she felt the pinch, and that was not magical at all. Sometimes its small fingers shaped like Yan Yan biscuit sticks would grab her finger and pull it into its toothless mouth. Instantly Cheryl would retract her finger, but like a siren, the baby wailed nonstop, teared like a broken faucet until she stuck it back into its mouth.

Cheryl would try anything to make it stop. She would stuff the pacifier into its mouth and rub its belly; she would pat it to sleep; she would carry it and walk around the house. She tried earplugs, loud music, soft music, sermons; but nothing could block out its deafening cries. Sometimes, out of desperation, she'd find herself whispering "Ooo ooo lah" and "Ah goo goo goo" at the doe-eyed face. Sometimes, when she caught herself doing that, she would put the baby back into its sarong and sing aloud what her grandmother used to sing to her: "Ong ah ong, ong kin kong. Kin kong kia…" She had to put the baby away; she could not bear the sight of its squishy face, its deep dimple—the stark resemblance to its father. The dimple gave the impression that it was smiling even when it was asleep, somehow still smiling through the sobs and screams. A steady happiness like that does not abate in grief or pain—but happiness at whose expense? Cheryl could not help but think of herself.

Sometimes, remembering that it had usurped all the good in her and stripped her of everything she thought herself to be, Cheryl would look at the baby with a saddened gravity, a weight so heavy that she had to tear the gaping mouth from her breast and plop down on the sofa bed where she had lain awake most of the nights. And each time she got up, she felt more burdened than she was before, as though the pain did not completely pass through but clung on to her heart.

The birth had ruined her. The doctor had cut her perineum and stitched her up and she was no longer the same. Cheryl lost the slender waist and the tight skin, her body gross and sagging; she had bled so much that she no longer recognised the stench of her blood. The baby, all because of the baby. Babies have that god-like power.

For a second Cheryl wished she could be as oblivious and powerful as a child again. The feeling of being young and unmindful was lost to her. Then she thought about the women in block D who were not allowed out. "Not D for Durian, okay? D for Dementia. D for Die," Judy Chua had said. Cheryl recalled the menacing tone and changed her mind. Instead she wished she could be like Baby Cheryl. That kid would have a great life in Canada, or anywhere as long as Clare was with her.

A bit flustered, but mentally intact and ready for tonight's party, Cheryl Dada resumed her life. She must get into the room, wash up and change, maybe pray for a smashing evening. As she was fumbling in her pocket for the door key, Cheryl Dada turned and saw the white bag hanging from the door beside hers. Jennifer was not at home; she was at her daughter's place. Her daughter and son-in-law had come on Sunday to sign her out for the week. She said she was staying over at their new apartment in River Valley that promised an unobstructed view of the fireworks. Good for her, thought Cheryl Dada, but she would rather stay in. It was Jennifer's loss that she was missing the party. How could she just take off like that? It was strange that she was thrilled about leaving, especially because she chose to be here. Like herself, Jennifer was a private case.

Rumour had it her daughter was going to take her out for good. Oi Leng from block C had overheard her asking Daniel about withdrawal procedures. Apparently Admission had no clue—they did not even know what the withdrawal request form looked like—so she stopped the head social worker in his tracks and tried him instead. But Daniel was just as clueless, stumbling over his words, taken aback by the request. In the end, it was Yu Yu who came to his rescue, referring her to Keng Boon who, having worked in the home for 20 years, must know what to do.

Repeating what she had heard from Yu Yu later, Oi Leng said that in order for residents to withdraw, even for those not serious case residents, the attending physician must complete a medical questionnaire and submit his evaluation. At this Oi Leng paused and had a look of hopelessness. "Don't need to leave liao," was her next remark. Cheryl was shocked that Oi Leng harboured the hope of leaving. Sure, she was the youngest among them, somewhere in her late thirties, though it was difficult to estimate age as there was something in the home, perhaps in the food or air, that seemed to interfere with the rate of degeneration.

Oi Leng was curvy, with a flat nose, fleshy lips and deep rosy cheeks. She had an excess of laughter and very dark hair—two undisputed signs of good health and well-being. To most people, Oi Leng was an unlikely resident. That was also Cheryl's query when they first met. But when they exchanged glances there it was. A dead giveaway: her left eye was made of acrylic. Oi Leng must have been keenly conscious of her half-blindness, for she usually wore sunglasses, except during therapy and meal times.

Having been here for so long, was she still hoping to be out there? For her own good, Cheryl thought, Oi Leng better perish any hope of leaving. She was certain that John Pitts, Dr Yang, Dr Smart, Dr Mahendran, the whole brood of them would never consent to signing anyone out of here. What were doctors for if there were no patients, no one to attend to? There was an order in the healthcare industry; everyone had a role to play.

It was bizarre to her that Oi Leng would have thought of leaving. What kind of life was she wishing for—a married life with a HDB flat, children and grandchildren? Oi Leng might have been single but she had three nieces who took turns to visit, always bringing things like mee chiang kueh and kueh salat with them. The single women in the home, or those who were widowed or who had never been in love, Cheryl thought, were the fortunate ones.

The question of singlehood made Cheryl think of Poh Choo, whose status was an enigma. According to Yu Yu, when Poh Choo had first arrived, she used to carry with her a black-and-white photograph of a man in uniform, which she would show to the residents and staff, and speak of him as though they were married. Mrs Rohan, her longest and best friend, corroborated this, adding that she would introduce the man as her sayang or ah lau, depending on whom she was talking to. Poh Choo, as one anecdote began, had in her sanest moment described how her sweetheart used to park his bicycle outside her kampong house. *Cring!*—that was their secret code. And she would run out to meet him—a Raffles boy, she apparently told Mrs Rohan. Poh Choo would laugh exultantly, retelling the story, her fists raised in the air to make a turning gesture, as though the bicycle were a scooter. Some residents thought the mystery man could be a brother; the sceptics reckoned he was a delusion. No one knew which version was true, for her longtime friend and the only insider to the story, Mrs Rohan, was also transferring out of block A to join Poh Choo next month.

Cheryl turned around, and she cast her eyes over the gated block that was diagonally across from where she was. Little was known about the residents of block D; some like Poh Choo were occasionally allowed out, but the severe cases never left their rooms. There was a rumour that the oldest resident was not Auntie Ng Ah Moon, who was bedbound in block C and on liquid feed, but actually an unnamed lady on the third floor of block D who was pushing 110 years. No one verified this. None of the women from the other blocks would reach out to the banished or probe further for fear of association with block D and its miasmic history. They had mistaken connection for relation and many good women were abandoned as a result, left to face their demons alone.

Poh Choo might still be hanging around the other blocks, saying hello and chatting with the women, but she was already regarded as stranger. Soon she would be a stranger to her best friend too. The anecdotes that would have helped her to uncover her past would also with the extrication of the last and only witness be reduced to hearsays, much like the black-and-white photograph that nobody saw again. Vanished and therefore impossible, the story was silenced and Poh Choo was mostly believed to be single.

Cheryl stopped herself at that thought. She, too, was guilty of doubting Poh Choo's story, guilty of cutting her off. Distractedly, she took a glance at her watch. It was almost six. There was not enough time for absolution today.

After a sigh, Cheryl lifted her head and turned her attention to the bag. "I guess Jennifer wouldn't mind," she said inaudibly. It's just a stupid bag. Jennifer did not need stickers or another Singa.

Looking around, certain that the corridor was clear, Cheryl slipped the strap of the bag off the doorknob and held the bag to her chest. Again she rummaged around thirstily, hoping to find Wally.

As she felt the inside of the bag and combed through the edges and curves of the memorabilia, hope began to dissipate, and the corners of her lips slowly dropped as she reflected on the meaning of the empty search. Slowly, Cheryl Dada hooked the bag back onto the doorknob and walked towards her room. In that half a minute or so, she thought about the party and another glimmer of hope came to her. There was still the door gift.

X

The room was bright and airy. Cheryl Dada drew the curtains and undressed herself. "Finally, we're alone together." The room welcomed her as she sat down on the bed. All she had wanted the whole day was some space for herself and air conditioning.

"I made it here," Cheryl Dada announced, looking round the spartan room, in awe of the solace. The quietude; the white paint; the four walls; the window with bars to fend off pigeons and stray cats; the view of the back garden. The most recent addition was the shelf on the wall that she had got Juwel to install. On it were some aged books; a thick wooden bookend kept them from falling off. Right in the middle of the shelf stood a red and silver Ultraman, arms crossed, tilted towards the empty, undusted spot where Singa Wally used to be. A long jade rosary lined the edge of the shelf like fairy lights.

It was a small and light, squarish room. Here, on the highest floor, Cheryl Dada felt in control of her life. More in control than on other days, she thought, lying down and adjusting her head on the pillow, to find the ceiling fan above her beginning to spin, slowly picking up speed. By force of habit her hand reached for the controls near the headboard and pushed the lever downwards. She looked at her legs rising, her toes twitching, as the bed made a humming sound, as the watch beeped twice. How fascinating it was, strange, even exhilarating to be able to do what she pleased, as if she now held the remote control for the life that was her own.

"Control," she uttered. The word toddled round the square room and came back to her devoid of meaning. Control was abjured when she let Adam slip the ring on her finger, which was now bony and swelled up at the joint; a pale strip ran around it, reminding her of the promise, her duty, a manacled life. I am Daughter. I am Wife. I am Mother. I am Grandmother, thought Cheryl Dada; the titles twisting into an invisible cord coiled around her neck, tipping her head up so she could look ahead and concentrate on the future. Was this the future her 13-year-old self had imagined? Ageing and arthritic, all alone in her room. A future without literature, except the seven books on her shelf that were foxed and dusty. She was quite done with the want to read more, write poems. That did not matter to her any more. Not when she was 51.

Supine, Cheryl raised her hand in the air, and peered through the spaces between her fingers, her eyes meeting the light emanating from the ceiling. As if beckoned by the bright presence, she closed her eyes and let out a long sigh of contentment. Her head sank deeper into the pillow. It's true what they said: a woman must have a room of her own. For Cheryl Dada it was the room on the fifth floor.

Cheryl rolled over to the edge of the bed to retrieve the small mirror from the drawer of the bedside table. Still lying down, she lifted the mirror and looked expectantly into it. The narrow face in the polished glass was dignified, with eyes fixed intently on her. She thought she would look older, more wrinkled, more sunken and indeed she was all of that, but the woman was above all serene, so serene that the marks of age receded. Chin slightly raised, the face revealed a resilience often confused with rebellion. Her jawline defined and eyebrows arched, there was nothing tentative about her. (She blinked slowly, revealing a twinkle in the round watery eyes; a fleeting glimpse of the girl who used to believe in the superstitions of religion and love.) Her hair, very much grey, fell into a luxurious sprawl across the pillow; it was a sagely kind of grey. Her lips, a deep red, were defined. Hers was a beauty without much makeup, a modesty that was incorruptible. If the woman in the glass looked haggard, it was because the necklace hanging loose round her neck revealed a thin throat. She made a mental note to wear a scarf to the party.

Cheryl Dada thought herself quite distinguished. More beautiful than the rest of them, she thought amusedly, shaking the mirror in her hand. She was tempted to say that she was the best-looking woman in the home. The other contender in her opinion was Cheng Hong but she was always in her room, allowing few to adore her natural beauty. Then again how would she know—what was the best? There were no explicit guidelines or judges to make the call. What is this elusive Best? In pre-U she was taught that the best is yet to be. The school's motto was a reminder that success in any form would not be final, that one must constantly strive to be better. "Our times are in His hand," said Browning. In Him who saith, "A whole I planned." This whole plan Cheryl assumed would manifest itself when she graduated. But even with straight As, she did not feel like she was the best. She had no idea what His plan was—whatever the best was.

When is Best going to come? Today, or tomorrow? The day after tomorrow? Is it always going to be a thing of tomorrow? Best is 30 years too late today. It's as much a myth as betterment, thought Cheryl Dada decidedly. To be better is what we tell ourselves so the Best is kept far away. Striving, striving, striving for the best made her tired and old. It's the whole hoping-is-living thing all over again. Hope has a funny way of creeping back into one's life. Looking once again into the mirror, she said to herself: "You are who I was: Cheryl Dada. And I am who you never wanted to be: Cheryl Dada."

Leaving her own face as eagerly as she had gone to find it, she put the mirror down on the bed. The clock on the wall read 6.10. It was time to change into the dress and pick out a suitable scarf.

Cheryl pulled herself up slowly. Sitting on her bed, she stared at the table, the foolscap paper, the pens lying around, the beige carver chair. This was where women became themselves, she thought—women who wrote alone in the room. She felt the letter in her pocket and the gravity of its words. She turned it over and over, raised her face towards it to trace the edges with her lips. After a minute or two Cheryl rose, walking over slowly to the table in her camisole, the red-stained letter in her hand, the murmurs of her feet rubbing across the marble floor.

She imagined, as she made her way towards the chair, what she might say to Sarah, and briefly entertained the thought that she might draw instead to avoid the intimidating precision of words. Two hands joined, from wrists to fingertips. No rings, no lines, no need for dimensions. Above her the fan was whirring as though in disagreement.

Cheryl sat on the low cushioned chair and placed the letter in the furthermost corner of the table. Flipping to a clean page on the foolscap pad, she scribbled a few lines, then scribbled some more. *Love gives hope so how can we not be drawn to hope?* She paused. *I cared for you in a simple way.* Pause. *I'm sorry.* Another pause. *If it were up to—*

Mrs Dada looked up, distracted; the tip of the pen was still on the page. In front of her was a wall decked with mostly photographs, some Polaroids hanging in a cluster and two postcards of the Niagara Falls.

There was a younger version of herself in a wedding dress with her mother standing beside her; the space between them had been erected as if to accommodate any last-minute addition to the picture. Cheryl leaned in to inspect her mother's face, but as soon as she began parsing the face, it became blotchy and holey, its contours melted into mush. At last she watched as the face dissolved and lost its shape, only the bulbous eyes pinned to the wall, watching, terrorising the lone woman since God knows when. She felt the menace, a sudden chill in the air. The eyes staring at her, unblinking.

Almost hysterical, Cheryl sprang off the chair and reached for the face, to rip the photograph off the wall; with determination and force, she dug her nails into the taunting face, scratching its eyes until the features became unrecognisable. Then both hands wrested the face from each other, half of her mother cast out the window, the other half crushed in the tight fist and chucked into the bin.

"Ah!" she gasped. Even in a room of her own, she was not left alone. Slouching against the windowsill, careful not to tip over the pot of cactus, Cheryl looked warily at the wall, her eyes scanning the remaining pictures. Nothing was amiss. She wondered if the Blu Tack would leave marks on the wall. Management said the room must be left in the state it was when she first moved in. But what could they really do when she was gone? She was no Lazarus, no coming back from the dead to give back a clean wall.

Finding the surroundings safe, Cheryl allowed herself to relax in the chair again. She had not realised that there was so much of Clare in the room: photos of Clare in her Tumble Tots shirt; Clare in diaper, on fours; Clare in diaper again, holding the telephone to her ear; Clare dressed up as a sheep in the nativity scene; Clare shaking the hands of some ang moh; Clare playing the piano; Clare wearing her softball glove and Crescent Girls' jersey—*DADA 12*; Clare at the zoo posing with Ah Meng; Clare at her 21st birthday party with people Cheryl did not recognise; Clare with a mortarboard on her head, the tassels blocking her eye from view; Clare with a tarantula on her shoulder; Clare in a diving suit, silver fish swirling around her; Clare in a beanie and scarf, sitting on a sleigh; Clare with a baby in her arms.

Cheryl examined the photographs, her finger feeling the tiny faces, the tanned faces, to find solidarity in each one as she saw semblances of herself in those fat cheeks, the round longing eyes, the collarbones visible beneath the thin shirt. It was strange to her that every photograph contained a bit of herself in it.

"Wah, pretty ah, your daughter. Same face leh," said the cleaning lady whenever she came to tidy the room; the other residents said the same. Only now was Cheryl Dada beginning to understand what people were saying. She used to think the girl looked more like Adam but it was really just the dimple on the cheek. Truthfully, Clare was nothing like her father; she did not inherit his compliance and contentment. And perhaps it was for the best. Cheryl conceded that it was true: Clare was so much like her, except that she was courageous.

Seated comfortably, Cheryl fixed her eyes on the photograph of Clare having breakfast with Ah Meng. The girl has no bone of fear in her, she mused smilingly, admitting to herself after 30 years of nonchalance that

Clare had been an accident she was now thankful for. And perhaps, because she was an accident, Clare learned to cherish the life that she had stumbled into. It seemed she had cried all her tears and sadness out when she was a baby, and that from the time she was a toddler she seldom shed a tear. She would fall from her tricycle and not cry, accidentally bite into a chili pod, wince and still would not cry. Once she almost drowned in the swimming pool and when Cheryl pulled her out Clare merely coughed and hastened to hug her mother.

Happy was her dominant mode. Cheryl did not understand her happiness but a cheerful child was easier to take care of. "Why is that girl always smiling?" her mother used to ask her. Because she took all of my hope, Cheryl wanted to say, but stopped herself. For she was guilty of the charge she had brought to her mother; she too had drained away all of her mother's hope.

Tracing with her thumb the wide grin that spread across Clare's face, Cheryl Dada was filled with hope. Yes, mother and daughter looked alike, but Clare had a different spirit. There wasn't for Clare, as there was for her, what she thought of as the worry of being left alone, cast out by the world. "I don't give a fuck, Mum," Clare had said repeatedly, and that was how she lived her life.

Cheryl pulled the chair closer to touch the photograph of Clare in her yellow and green jersey. *MUM, WE WON! WE ARE THE CHAMPIONS... WE ARE THE CHAMPIONS...* The letters in black ink lined the white rim of the instant film. She had acquired a tan and her hair was already short. Must have been secondary three, Cheryl deduced from the piercings on her ear, and wiped away the grime on the photograph to get a better look.

The three earrings dangling from her ear and the one sticking out of her nose had got the girl into trouble with the discipline mistress in school. It also caused a cold war between Clare and Adam that lasted for weeks; Clare refusing to talk to him, Adam withholding her allowance. Cheryl stayed clear of the father-daughter conflict. She was the parent cheering on the side line, occasionally handing a $10 note to Clare. She would not chime in, though she knew Adam was desperate for support and validation; her silence had undermined him time after time. The truth was that Cheryl thought herself incapable of mothering. Why, it seemed but yesterday that she herself was little more than a girl in secondary school.

She thought they both had no right to decide what was good for Clare. Even Clare could not have known what was good for herself. No, not at that age. So Cheryl recused herself, either absent in person or spirit, when it came to making decisions, mostly unhelpful in parenting, choosing indifference so that she was the least influential in shaping Clare's life. She would have wanted that for herself too, for her mother to have left her alone.

Without Cheryl's meddling, Clare had turned out to be champion indeed, unconcerned about what her father and everyone else thought, only remorselessly following her instincts. It seemed to Cheryl that humans sometimes needed to be elemental—that is, to let go of civilities and considerations of consequences. She could not do it; she was not savage enough to confront her primal needs. But Clare, the pitcher with the most home runs on the team, trusted herself to deliver her thoughts and wishes with ferocity and defended what she stood for even when the odds were stacked against her. So that was what it meant to not give a fuck about anything but oneself.

What is she hopeful about? Cheryl thought, and her thumb glided over to the next photograph and paused at the edge of Clare's lips. Hers was a smile without teeth, the right amount of cheekiness, the kind that accentuated the fullness of the lips. She looks good in red, Cheryl thought wistfully, referring to the lipstick Clare had put on for the graduation photoshoot. Cheryl also thought that Clare did not need the red to accentuate her smile. Be it Ah Meng by her side or a tarantula on her shoulder, she would still be smiling. It was incomprehensible, her having no fear whatsoever.

Even when she was a foetus, Clare did not give a fuck, Cheryl thought, remembering the day at Mount Alvernia, the day of the reveal. She propped herself up and arose from the chair, suddenly breaking into a chuckle, as she recalled how the doctor had told her that the baby was a boy, then said it was a girl; that he had mistaken her finger for a penis.

The thought of Clare giving men the finger when she was just the size of a grapefruit amused her now, but back then having a girl was the second worst possible news Cheryl had received in three months.

At first she could not believe it even though all three sticks had two lines and her period was late. But there was no use doubting the doctor's report that so thoroughly mapped out the future for her. She was to quit school and stay home.

Cheryl Dada waited for a long time. She kept on waiting but anticipation and excitement never came. Was the thing in her belly really the miracle of life? She had heard so much about the baby's first kick but when it happened it felt like a scene from *The Fly*. Horror! Horror! "Oh God, please take it away!" she cried out in the hospital toilet. "Please! Just this one time, please!" she begged. It cannot be, it cannot! She was not yet an adult; she was still in school! Oh how she screamed in the cubicle, lifting her head as far back as she could, trying to get her eyes away from the bump that was her belly.

Did other women feel the same? she wondered, turning her attention to the photograph of Clare and Baby Cheryl, who was just a couple of days old here, swaddled in a green polka dot blanket. It must be that she had not one maternal bone in her. Eight months passed and still she felt no motherly instincts.

Cheryl gave up on waiting. She knew she could not love what she did not want, neither could she give her life to it, so she decided to do the bare minimum. She would meet the baby's physical needs—comfort and hunger. It was always fed, powdered, cleaned and dressed; but Cheryl would not coo or sing to it, never consciously. Many times she reminded herself that she would give what she could but no more, because what is given is given away. Motherhood isn't the same as martyrdom. She had seen her mother give when she had nothing to give and take back what she had given. The whole business of giving and taking made her miserable. If a mother's love was that, Cheryl wanted no part in it. She wanted to be nothing like her mother.

Clare wasn't like her mother either, she thought with relief and gratitude. Unlike the women in her family, Clare would survive the world and its injustices. Cheryl walked around the room, from the table to the bed, pausing at the wardrobe to brush her hand against the red dress for tonight's party, then walked around some more, thinking about Mama the matriarch; her mother the Nonya who had married outside the community, who used the blender instead of the lesung; and she, Cheryl, the third generation one-quarter Nonya who could not speak Malay. Clare did not care about being part Peranakan and was unburdened by its demands. She only liked the part of the culture where women ruled the family, but attributed the female reign to runaway fathers and men of poor health. It was the lack of male presence, not independence and defiance, which had earned her grandmother the titular head of the family. Peranakan matriarchy, Clare would tell her mother, was an insidious form of domesticity that pretended to empower women within the home so as to keep them away from potential freedom outside. She said the Little Nonya was the Malayan Angel in the House.

Standing in the middle of the room on the top of the home, Cheryl wondered if she was one of those angels that Clare spoke against. The thought of having soft feathery wings was somewhat pleasing to her. Though she seldom understood her daughter's criticisms, she admired her passion. Clare was outspoken and always teaching her new words like "butch", which means a type of masculine woman, and "trans-", which she explained means "across". Like how Cheryl was at present *trans*-ing her room to get to the bed. Adam, however, did not appreciate Clare's insights as much as Cheryl did, choosing to interpret her tone and indignation as disrespect.

He was seldom interested in Clare's ideas, Cheryl thought, as she reached to touch the velvety sheets of the bed. He wasn't intelligent enough to argue with her either. For a quick moment, Adam's face, which often deepened into a disapproving frown when Clare spoke, flashed before Cheryl. She tried to shrug it off, quickly resting herself in the bed.

Cheryl knew some part of him came very near to resenting them for not living up to his expectations even though it was not in his nature to be bitter. He thought himself more saintly than that. Adam's world was rosy and strait-laced; his vantage point was higher than Cheryl and Clare's. He could not see the world the way they tried to explain things to him.

In his eyes both daughter and mother had failed him. Adam would never confront her but he blamed Cheryl for Clare. What mother brings a child into the world and leaves it? It was unnatural; she was unnatural. He said she was carrying her womb in her head. He said being a mother was a heart thing, not a mind game. He said all of that with an inflection used by accusers. Of course, Cheryl knew that. There was nothing fun about pregnancy, childbirth or sex, for that matter. She was not playing games when she refused to nurse the baby. She was also not pretending to sleep when it kept crying in the night.

The memory of the accusation nailed Cheryl to the bed.

"Not all women are the same," she whispered to herself, pulling the blanket to her neck as the evening breeze settled in the room. "Today is my birthday. I am not who I was last year. I'm not who I was before coming to this place." Cheryl was calm. The air was cool, and the room was peaceful.

Nestled in the bed, she lay comfortably, overcome with gratefulness for the home. It was true, she had many issues with Management, she abhorred some of the nurses and kitchen staff especially, but the home afforded her and the women freedom to be who they wanted to be without the scrutiny of their loved ones.

Cheryl thought of Choon Eng, Mrs Rohan, Loudspeaker Leow, Judy Chua, Siew Eng, Felicia, Poh Choo, Oi Leng, Gina and Gracie Koh...women who, if not for this place, would have nowhere to go. Women like herself and Cheng Hong would have been cut into slices by their very own hands.

What of Cheng Hong and her afflictions? Cheryl lingered on the thought of her. If they had more opportunities to chat, if she came down to the dining hall more often, they could perhaps be friends who had a fair foundation based on their conditions of ugly wrists and weak hearts.

Cheryl felt herself sinking further into the softness of the sagging bed. Even though they did not have meandering conversations, and almost always haggled over TV room rights and the karaoke microphone, the women had a common understanding that they were in the home together—for as long as they lived. Leaving was not an option, they understood this.

When they were granted admission, they were sworn into a sorority of reclusive and cantankerous women. Signing the indemnity and declaration forms, they had pledged loyalty to the holy circle of trust ringed by the picket fences of the home. No one had to explain themselves; their histories were unimportant and made terrible dinner conversations. Some women were quieter than others; some, like Loudspeaker Leow and Judy Chua, were more rambunctious and angry. Some of them were widows; a few were divorcees. But majority of them were mothers. Some were mothers without children, some were mothers left here by their children. Most were, by now, disenchanted by motherhood.

What men like Adam did not understand was that motherhood was not for every woman. Because she could not find maternity in her heart, Cheryl had to figure it with her mind. Breastfeeding, changing diapers, telling bedtime stories, childproofing the house, blowing on hot food—these did not come naturally to her. And she thought it was disgusting to feed Clare with the food that she had cooled in her mouth, the bits she had chewed up and spat on the plate. The doctor and Adam told Cheryl that she needed time to get used to the idea of motherhood and she should be patient. But it wasn't just time. The idea of nursing was repulsive to her. So, yes, Adam was right; her mother was right. Her way of mothering was unnatural. Motherhood was unnatural to her too.

What more did they want from her? Born in 1965, she was the nation's child; its poster girl; the sign on the female toilet door; the *F* in the NRIC. She was her mother's last resort, a hope for her crumbling marriage, a surrogate for her stillborn; she was Adam's wife and the love of his life. They took her mind, her heart, her life, and they had taken her womb. Child of God or not, her mother had told her to keep the baby; Adam pleaded with her. She would have said no. But no, nobody asked her what she wanted. If she were honest back then, would it have made any difference? To her? To Adam? To Clare?

Love was the panacea. It was supposed to bind them all together. A bloody love, love that was from within, flowing in the veins, connecting all of them. They call it family. Adam and Clare were family. And the baby too. Adam, Clare and the baby, she repeated to herself. Adam. Clare. Baby. She said louder with increasing bite: "ADAM,

CLARE, BABY. ADAM! CLARE! BABY!" She spat them out, name by name, until the words attached themselves to the corners of the room, until her breathing shortened.

Cheryl turned to her side, and turned again. Her eyes scanned the room and stayed on the bit of the ceiling where the slender scarlet cord hung steadfastly. Did Rahab think she was going to be part of the royal genealogy when she tied the red rope to the window? Did it really matter who our foremothers were—harlot or Pharisee? Cheryl thought of her mother, the godly woman who seldom withdrew the rod of discipline; the lacerated face that was resting somewhere in Mrs Rohan's lawn. She was family; thick blood banded them together. But Cheryl must not let her mind go there; she must not call out her name. The trouble with her mother was not the remembering part; it was the forgetting. Cheryl could still see her head shaking, the rotan with the pink hook in her hand flailing in the air, the croaky voice screaming, "You're an abomination!"

She turned again, this time with more effort, unable to elude the scene that was replaying in her mind. She saw the wooden stick raised and lurching forwards, striking once, twice, thrice; the skin turning more crimson with each whip. Her arm was pulsing, the skin flashing red, as if it had a heart of its own, separate from the benumbed muscle caged in her chest.

Thud! The rotan struck, and struck another time. Her arm was steady like a shield, pushing against the force of each stroke, refusing to be broken by the stick-thin adversary. Although Cheryl could not help the tears that were running down her cheeks, her arm was faithful.

At last the end of the rotan was fraying; some splinters were left in the swollen skin. Then the rotan was back on the wall, and it did not hurt any more.

"You're not an abomination," Cheryl whispered to her bruised arm, gently smearing aloe vera gel over it. Curled up under the study desk in her room, she heard the voice wailing, "God, how come she is like that? God, deliver us from our sins!" It was quiet for a moment, then it would start again, "God, why? Oh forgive her!" She begged on. "Lord, she knows not what she has done!" The intercessions were loud and grating, and after a while it was just noise.

When the room darkened, Cheryl crawled up into the bed. She held the white rabbit to her chest. "We're not an abomination," she said to Doraemon, pulling him to her right side. "Do not fear, for the Lord is with us," she told Ultraman, whose hands were held together as if giving benediction. She pulled the duvet over her head and mumbled a short prayer into the palm of her unhurt hand, wishing that God would listen this time. She squeezed her eyes shut and secretly hoped tomorrow won't come.

Cheryl had a bad night, and the next day was worse. She remembered waking up in the morning to the sound of the telephone ringing and her mother shouting in the living room. When she opened her eyes, she saw that Doraemon's pouch was stained and the bedsheet was red. Her arm was sore and her tummy hurt a lot. The feelings that had inundated her that morning seemed to have diffused into the present. Cheryl's arms were stiff and heavy; the hurt from the beating was resurging.

Many things happened that morning. It was the first time Cheryl felt a sudden drop in energy from the loss of girlhood, a mood-sapping lethargy that only women understood. She remembered what she had learned in Sunday school the week before and immediately associated her predicament with that of the Israelites who were slain at Mount Sinai just after God had delivered them. The sharp descent from high hopes to the lowest of valleys, the fall from grace—what she knew in her head and memory she experienced with the entirety of her body that morning. It was also the first time she realised that the happiness she wanted could make her unhappy because it was not her own. Happiness was not free. It was society's, it was her mother's. So Cheryl would rather the lesser happiness. It seemed better for her to be unhappy, because while nobody was eager to plunge into the profundity of grief, preferring the don't-ask-don't-tell approach, everyone wanted to partake in joy. Happiness had to be shared. Grief, on the other hand, was singular, and could stay unstirred for years.

How odd to be happy and sad at the same time, Cheryl thought, replaying the events of that morning. She was happy when her mother told her that she did not have to go to school any more, then it pained her to think that she could not see Sarah again, more painful than the swollen lines on her arm, and later still, for many years ahead, sadness prevailed. From that day on, her feelings were muddled up, her thoughts were confusing, her entire life was a mess.

Even now Cheryl wasn't sure what to feel about herself and about the unfinished letter that was sitting on the table. She wanted to go back to it but her shoulders had stiffened; her fingers would not wiggle.

Cheryl Dada tried to lift her head from the pillow but she could not feel her neck. Her body was tense and resistant, not seeming to belong to her. She knew she ought to be disturbed by this sensation or the lack thereof, but she could not make herself care enough to pull the scarlet cord or push the knob on the side of the bed.

Instead Cheryl Dada thought about all the things that mattered to her. She had wanted a normal family and the love that would assure her that there was still a unit of good in the world. She tried to do the right thing and made sure her new family was nothing like the one she had had: a father who had died before she could call him Pa and a mother whose life's mission was to forget that she had a daughter—and it wasn't like that at all, thankfully. But it wasn't better either. She could not bring herself to love Adam; and Clare, who preferred women, was moving away to Toronto. For most of her life Cheryl Dada wanted love and she almost had it. She also wanted expression but there was no one to talk to. Suddenly impassioned, she let herself admit that all she really wanted was Sarah.

She saw her hands tightly clenching the fabric of her pinafore. Sarah would not look at her; her eyes were cast down, fixed upon the concrete floor. She would have darted out of the cubicle if not for Cheryl who was backed up against the door, Cheryl who had hurt her with the arrow of shame.

Cheryl shut her eyes to see Sarah in the blue uniform still. She was sullen, embarrassed, perplexed by the restraint that she misunderstood for revulsion. And rightly so, for Sarah, who was only acquainted with the tickling sensations of the heart, could not have understood the moderation of feelings that Cheryl was learning every Sunday.

So when Cheryl started weeping, her tears falling between their cheeks, Sarah pulled away from the reluctant lips to see in the eyes of her favourite friend an expression of pain. The eyes that would narrow when her fingers reached deep into her were tearing up and would not stop. It was an expression she could only associate with the look on the faces of those who had done something wrong and irrevocable, like her mischievous brothers who were frequently caned by Ma, or schoolmates who were made to squat in the field for playing truant; and Sarah felt guilty by association, by looking at Cheryl.

Joy infected with shame was something the prelapsarian youth did not understand. It was either flight or fondling for her, and since Cheryl was reticent, Sarah withdrew reactively; her hand slipped away from under her friend's dress and backed into the desolation of her own pocket.

In those few moments, the girls stood motionless, their eyes no longer gazing into each other's. Between them was a great vastness and Cheryl knew no amount of words would draw them close. At last, as the bell for the end of recess came and went, seven seconds in total, Cheryl threw herself out recklessly into the shadows of the fateful afternoon towards the cataleptic figure. The bodies, one boyish and the other delicate, folded into each other. The hems of their blue dresses joined. The teenagers held on wordlessly. In the silence, the things that could neither be uttered nor asked wove round them and pulled them closer, before finally wisping away.

Cheryl peered a long moment into the room. If I had said something, she thought; if I had persevered. Would it have changed things? And then she thought: if only they had the words for what they felt...

But now that she knew what the words were, what could she possibly say to change things? The letter was writing its conclusion in her mind with pleasantries and clichés. *Happy National Day! Write to me often. When are you coming back? Are you mar*— The words that would express what she really felt were left unmanned in her heart, going in all directions but unable to be articulated.

It wasn't just love, Cheryl contemplated, and stopped trying to turn in the bed. She gave in to the stiffness of her body, hoping inaction would afford her the energy to focus on the memory of Sarah. Surely not everything has to do with love. Whatever it was—friendship, the intimacy between women, puppy love, infatuation, true love—she never gave it a chance. What tragedy implicit in the affection was never enacted. Her regret was not trying hard enough, not trying at all. She told herself that she could not have done anything even if she wanted to, that she was too young, that she was born in the wrong time, that it was her mother's fault. All of that was true, and Cheryl wished she could be persuaded by the facts. But the only bit of the story that kept clawing at her was the one about her walking away from something that actually mattered to her. It seemed she was always thinking about that.

At 13 she had surrendered. She went into hiding when she should have hit back, silent against her wants, thinking that her feelings would somehow go away—with a boyfriend perhaps, and more assuredly with Time—not knowing that obedience meant complicity. She had walked away from something that she would never discover again. From then on her life seemed to be a search for different sorts of emotional attachments to make up for the deficit. She tried the softball team, she tried to make friends, she tried men. She waited. And when the opportunity came to rebel against all that her mother stood for, Cheryl took it right away. She knew she had ripped out her mother's heart but she revelled in her mother's pain. Never had she felt closer to her: it was a necessary agony, one that allowed her to sympathise with her mother, for it was only via sympathy that she could feel something for the woman who had given birth to her.

Cheryl thought she had won. Then the pregnancy happened. Then the wedding. At 20 she was still in debt. She was still losing, losing more—for this time she had given her flesh and blood away which from conception was no longer hers. It was a Dada: the family's signature imprinted on the baby's left cheek. All these years the debt was chasing her nonstop, reminding her of the night she crouched in her room, the night she took him in, the night the baby arrived.

"My God, what have I done!" she burst out, and tried to hold in the beads of tears forming underneath her lashes, although her hands could not move, could not dry her face. Cheryl wept for herself, silently and alone in the room, mourning the amputation. She thought about all the missed opportunities and indecisions that had shaped her life. "My God!" she exclaimed, as the last of her tears fell to the pillow.

But, but maybe, she thought, just maybe there is still time. At 51 I still can— Those nights...those nights are nothing compared to tonight! Maybe I have done what I can undo, she thought, her eyes agleam with a faint light.

If at 13 she had been more firm with her mother, just like how she was with the staff about the table decorations and menu, things would probably pan out differently. If her mother were here in the room, she would say to her, "No, I don't want to go to another school." She would have told her mother that there was nothing wrong with her. If at 13 she had said no to her mother, things would be different. She would still be single, still searching perhaps, but definitely more fulfilled than now. She might have even finished school and gone on to do a Masters like Clare did.

But her mother was gone. "She's gone to be with the Lord," the quaking voice had said over the telephone. Gone, it said; not asleep. Not raptured, as her mother would have liked.

Cheryl thought of the things she had forgotten to tell her mother. That she wished her mother had had a miscarriage the second time around so they could all have been spared from this freak show; that she wished she wasn't like her. She might have told her that she lost her virginity and married out of spite because she did not want to be that fucking white flower. She might have apologised to her mother, but for what? No, she did not regret not being there when she died. No, she did not regret sending her to St Mary's. It was a holy place where old folks said grace before meals and had prayer service every other evening. If anything, Cheryl regretted not having sent her there earlier. She should have done so the moment the symptoms were showing. It was a lesson learned in the hardest way. Unlike her mother, she would not allow herself to die without dignity. Symptoms or not, hereditary or not, after her mother's death Cheryl felt a distinct and urgent necessity to find a place of her own and, lo and behold, Elderflower Nursing Home on Avenue 7 had vacancies. So she checked in as soon as she settled her mother's funeral and finances. The sale of her mother's flat had fetched her some money that bought Cheryl a permanent room in Elderflower. It was her decision; it was for her best.

And Adam and Clare did not have to feel bad about her living in the home. Just like she did not have to feel bad about her mother.

Cheryl wished she cared more. She wished she felt something but she could not bring herself to follow Adam and Clare to the hospital. There was not enough anger, bitterness, sympathy or anything strong enough to get her out of the house. She felt nothing for her mother.

But what Cheryl really wanted to tell her mother, even though she could never say it out, was that she understood. That she knew why she had done what she did. Like Cheryl, her mother had been clueless and young, pregnant at 20, half-hearted about marriage, feral in old age, forever grappling with the inconsistencies of life. Cheryl had chosen differently; but she could have easily done the same. Her mother had gone before her and tried one route, so Cheryl knew not to follow. The woman had stuck it out; she stayed as long as she could till the end. But back then Cheryl did not know better. Now she saw the routes clearly: both ways led to the same place. She understood that her mother had tried. And that was good enough for Cheryl.

Thinking about these things, Cheryl became keenly aware of how bogged down she was. Her body had become heavy, lodged in the bed. It was as if her blood had thickened and her organs were bricks. Was it the protracted effect of the medicine? She blew out a long breath and the ceiling seemed to breathe back at her. Something was pressing on her eyelids.

Grounded in the bed, unable to move, she was some solid object with a leaden heart, limbs and parts like blocks attached to the body by a carpenter. If life were metrical, she was feeling it now, all 51 years of dead weight and more. The albatross on her chest was here to stay, its talons dug deep. This must be what it feels like to be antique, Cheryl Dada thought, as she gave a big yawn. At least she could still feel her face.

Cheryl wondered if there was time for a nap. She could really use some rest. She wanted to close her eyes, to stop thinking about the past. The heavy body secured her to the bed; but it did not stop her prodigal heart and mind from their reckless, wandering ways. They seem to be growing and growing, thoughts and feelings uncontrollable and in excess, until they pressed on the white walls, blindly feeling for an exit.

Cheryl had to get out. It was really time to change; the party was starting soon. The red dress matched with a crystal waist belt were waiting for her. (Lulu had done a remarkable job of ironing the dress; it was difficult to get crinkles out of chiffon.) As much as Cheryl wanted to wear it, it seemed impossible that the clothing would fit this antique body of hers. She felt that the arms resting by her sides had become swollen, hard and bulky like Clare's softball bats.

She willed them to move but only some fingers curved upwards. Her body was reluctant to rise. It seemed to have sunk deep into the bed. The entire day had taken its toll on Cheryl Dada; the long hours of thinking and feeling about the past 51 years. She thought of the black sofa and her father. Maybe it was time to let go. She remembered her grandmother had said that he went in peace and was probably in heaven with God. Probably did not even see death coming in the form of the taxi that was charging towards him. Maybe it was time to let the body take over. Her heart and mind had hardly worked to her advantage, so why not try the body at this hour? If it was bent on lying down, then she must not fight its will. Maybe it was time to rest. In the room, her body stretched out on the bed, she was moored; she was cool; she was ready.

Outside the room was nothing. No one lived above her, only the blazing sun that had disappeared from the dimming sky, day blending into night. Life was harsh out there: the heat of the day, the haze, the humidity. And there was the hullabaloo. What was the racket? What were they talking about?

The party must be starting. Cheryl heard a male voice—it was Adam's. Was he talking to Judy Chua? She was gabbling about something petty again. The shrill voice stuck out among the sounds of patriotic songs and the clanging of bowls and plates. Loudspeaker Leow was deafening as usual, fanning so-and-so's grievance. There were other voices too; most were female and old-sounding. The strident voices travelled through the half-open windows, carrying bits of conversations: "I din see her today—" "You got see the flag just now?" "You got see the ang pow how much?" "Wah this year big budget you know." "I saw the plane fly leh! Got five fighter planes!" "Got meh—" "Who say?" "Who—" Then there was a lull in the noise, and a disembodied voice ejected: "Minister come already!"

Everyone rose. The VIPs, the residents and their healthcare aides; Lulu and Vikash, who were standing at the back; Adam, who was bothering John with his questions; Daniel and Ling Na, who were shuttling between the reception and kitchen. The crowd came to a standstill; all eyes were fixed on the man on the stage. Juwel was not there (he was on his way to some multi-storey car park), but he would hear from the rest of them tomorrow that the party had been smashing.

As the crowd clapped, Cheryl saw herself getting changed and heading downstairs. She would appear in her red dress, tall and ravishing, just before the applause died down. They would turn and there she was. They would be enthralled by her presence; they would say, "It is Cheryl Dada."

But first she had to get up. Cheryl fidgeted on the bed, loosening the nails of age. Tonight was her night, she was not going to miss the party. She shifted her weight from side to side and her muscles finally began to relax. She yawned and tried to bring her hands to her tearing eyes. Her hands were trembling but slowly made it up to her face.

Cheryl Dada was trying; but she was interrupted again. A sound moved her. A melodious sound crescendoing from under the pillow filled the room: "She loves you, yeah, yeah, yeah. She loves you, yeah, yeah, yeah. She loves you, yeah, yeah, yeah, yeahhhhh…"

It was their favourite song. She used to sing it to her: "She loves you, yeah, yeah, yeah—" Clare would ask, "Who loves me, Mum?" And Cheryl would kiss her, hoping she would understand without words. The melody led her hand into the sheets. From under the pillow she reached and pulled out the tablet. With effort Cheryl turned her head and saw the face smiling at her. She smiled back and opened her mouth, as if to say something. The face continued smiling. Paul, George and John were singing: "She loves you, yeah, yeah, yeah…"

Cheryl let her weary fingers wander over the face; she was moved by its hopefulness. They paused over the red lips that curved in the happiest kind of way; and she knew the smile. A sense of peace fluttered over her. She was finally ready.

"She loves you, yeah…"

The ringing stopped. It was quiet for a moment. Then the watch beeped twice. The fingers that held the face stopped trembling. They slackened, and the tablet rested on the bed. On the screen the face twitched, the smile fading. The red lips began to part.

ABOUT THE AUTHOR

Carissa Foo received her Ph.D. in English Studies from Durham University and is currently teaching at Yale–NUS College. Apart from her research interest in modernist women's writing, she also teaches conversational English to migrant workers. *If It Were Up To Mrs Dada* is her first novel.

ACKNOWLEDGEMENTS

I am grateful to Angela Frattarola who showed me the beauty of moments. For help with the manuscript, I must thank Sheri. Many thanks to Edmund for his faith in local stories.

I am blessed to have family and friends who make every step on this earth lighter. Special thanks to Conny, Jun, Mitch, and the earliest readers: Dippy, Cheryl, Xiaohui. Not forgetting God who first loved me.